THE BATTLE FOR TEXAS

ROBERT VAUGHAN

WOLFPACK
PUBLISHING
— EST 2013 —

The Battle for Texas
Paperback Edition
© Copyright 2021 (As Revised) Robert Vaughan

Wolfpack Publishing
5130 S. Fort Apache Rd. 215-380
Las Vegas, NV 89148

wolfpackpublishing.com

Paperback ISBN 978-1-64734-760-4
eBook ISBN 978-1-64734-759-8

THE BATTLE FOR TEXAS

Chapter 1

The settlement was so temporary that it didn't even have a name. It hugged the Texas side of the Sabine River, the first settlement in the new country, on the trail of El Camino Real, the Road of Kings. The little town was no more than a cluster of canvas tents, a few huts thatched with reeds from the canebrake, and one or two wagons that had been abandoned by earlier travelers moving west.

The biggest tent belonged to a man named Lightfoot. He sold liquor there, and men gathered there, to play cards and other games of chance. Few goods and services could be purchased with money, so currency had lost much of its value. As a result, it was not unusual for the men to play for stakes that would have intimidated the most daring gamblers in the gaming halls of New Orleans.

A few hundred yards away from the settlement, Luke Calhoun lay asleep in the canebrake. The rushes grew to heights of ten feet, curving over at the top to form leafy caves and corridors to blot out the sun. If one chose a spot carefully, one could sleep throughout the day without being awakened by sunshine or disturbed by passersby.

Luke was sleeping in such a spot, though he didn't remember choosing it. He had gambled too hard and drunk too much the night before and, when he left Lightfoot's establishment, he had somehow wound up among the cane.

There was a gunshot not ten feet from Luke's head and he sat up immediately.

"Did you git 'im, Nate?" a voice yelled.

"No." The answering voice was very close to Luke but the thick cane prevented him from seeing the other two men. "Leastwise, I don't think I did," the second voice said. "It's hard to tell."

"I told you it don't make no sense to hunt rabbit in the canebrake. Even iffen you was to get one, more'n likely he'd hop off in the rushes and you'd lose him. Come on, let's go down to the riverbank and git us a big ol' catfish." Luke heard the crashing of cane as the two hunters left the rushes to return to the settlement.

Luke picked up his hat and put it on, covering hair the color of ripe wheat. He stood up and stretched, and the action revealed that he was nearly six feet tall with a muscular chest, narrow waist and hips, and broad shoulders. He heard a soft rustling sound and turned to see a rabbit looking out at him from behind a clump of cane. Luke smiled and his amber eyes twinkled.

"You gave those two fellas a pretty good run, didn't you?" he said quietly. "You also woke me up. I ought to shoot you and eat you for breakfast."

As if he could understand the words, the rabbit turned and darted quickly away.

Luke's mouth was dry from too much drink the night before. He was not normally given to drinking to excess but, on his last trip west, he had seen a sight he wanted desperately to forget. He had arrived at the settlement the day before and he spent last night trying to blot the vision from his mind forever.

It hadn't worked. He had a terrible headache, an awful taste in his mouth, a queasy stomach, and when he closed his eyes, he could still see the dismembered bodies of Ethan Cox, his wife, and their little boy and girl.

Luke had passed a night in the Cox cabin on his way out and he had killed a deer and left it with them in thanks for their hospitality. Now, they were all dead.

When Luke first saw them, he thought they had been murdered by a marauding band of Indians but Luke could read sign as well as the average person could read a newspaper. It took him no time at all to realize that the Cox massacre was the work of renegade soldiers. Whether they were Mexicans or Texans, he couldn't tell. He knew that it might even be a mixed band, for when soldiers went bad, they sometimes banded together in an unholy alliance, swearing allegiance to no one.

Luke walked out of the canebrake and into the clearing. There was a meeting going on among the people who had recently arrived from the East in half a dozen wagons. They were the first wagons of a train that was forming to go on to Austin but, until it was large enough to defend itself against Indian raids, the wagon train would stay in the settlement. There were a dozen fires, some for cooking, and some for heating water for laundry. A group had gathered in front of Lightfoot's tent to watch a cockfight. For a settlement with no name, this place was taking on all the amenities of a real town.

Luke walked to the riverbank and got down on his hands and knees to drink and wash his face and hands. He soaked his hat in the cool water before he put it back on. Not until then did he begin to wake up and realize that he was hungry. He stuck his hands in his pockets to see if he had enough money to buy some food from one of the settlers' wives. Most of them were willing to set a meal for a stranger for fifteen cents and some had earned enough money that way to help their husbands get together a grubstake for their new start.

Luke couldn't find two coins to rub together. "You son of a bitch!" a low, menacing voice said.

The hair on the back of Luke's neck stood up and he felt his pulse quicken and his muscles tingle. He didn't know who had addressed him, or why the man had spoken in such a way, but he sensed the threat in the words.

"Turn around, you bastard," the low voice continued. "I want you to see the man who's going to send you to hell!" Luke turned slowly and looked up to the top of the shallow embankment by the river's edge. There stood the biggest man he had ever seen. He looked to be at least six feet eight inches tall and weighed nearly three hundred pounds. He was dressed in farmer's homespun and he wore chin whiskers. From the top of the rise, he was staring at

Luke down the barrel of a long, ugly rifle. He raised the rifle to his shoulder.

Luke saw the farmer pull back the hammer and aim the rifle. Luke fell to one side, into the river, just as the gun roared. The rifle ball whipped past him with an angry buzz and slapped heavily into the water A large cloud of smoke billowed out from the discharged weapon.

"I missed, dammit!" The big man cursed and then quickly pulled his powder horn around to reload.

Luke didn't give him a chance to fire again. He waded out of the water and climbed the riverbank toward the farmer. The man was holding the rifle loosely between his knees as he poured powder out of the horn. Luke grabbed the weapon and threw it to one side but the farmer, with another curse, swung at him.

Luke ducked under the big man's wild swing and that put him into position to throw his own punch. He was well set and he put all of his power behind his swing. He hit the farmer square on the nose and felt it break under his fist.

The big man let out a bellow, more in anger than in pain, but he didn't go down. Instead, he reached out with both arms. Luke knew that if the man got him in a bear hug, he could squeeze the life out of him.

The farmer was much larger than Luke, though Luke himself was a big man. Luke had the advantage in agility, if not strength, and he used it to avoid the farmer's rush. The man found himself off balance and Luke used the man's own momentum to send him tumbling down the embankment and into the water. By the time the man came up, sputtering and spitting,

Luke had his pistol pointed at him. The man saw the gun and stopped, staring up at him, still defiant, but no longer fighting. By now, nearly everyone in the settlement had been drawn to the scene, first by the gunshot and then by the fistfight. They laughed at the spectacle of the big man dripping water.

"All right, you got the drop on me, mister. Go ahead and kill me. Get it over with," the farmer said.

"Who the hell are you and why did you try to kill me?" Luke asked. He put his pistol back in his holster.

"I'm Florrie's husband," the man said.

"I don't know any Florrie."

"Mister are you goin' to add lyin' to your sin of adultery?" the farmer asked. "Are you tellin' me you don't remember the woman you was with in Natchitoches?"

"Oh, *that* woman," Luke said.

"Oh, *that* woman," someone in the crowd mimicked and everyone laughed uproariously.

"I never learned her name," Luke said.

"That makes it even worse!" the farmer said.

Luke extended his hand to help the farmer climb out of the water. "I'm sorry," he said, quietly. "I didn't know she was married. She, uh, didn't act like she was married," he added undiplomatically.

In fact, the only woman he'd had anything to do with in Natchitoches had been a bar girl who charged him for her services.

The farmer sighed. "I know," he said. He wrung out his hat, put it back on, and stood quietly for a moment. The crowd, realizing there would be no more fighting, began to go back to whatever they had been doing before, and Luke and the big man were left alone. "I guess I've made a fool of myself. It weren't your fault. You took her for just what she is—a whore. It ain't you I should be goin' after. It's *her*."

"If you want my opinion, you don't have any business going after *her*, either," Luke said.

"You mean I should just stand by and let her make a fool of me?"

"Did you know what she was when you married her?"

"Yeah, I knew."

"Seems to me like you only have two choices," Luke said. "You either take her like she is or you just walk away and leave her be."

"I know," the farmer said. "But it's hard on a man's pride, you know what I mean? She's as purty a little thing as I ever laid eyes on and there ain't that many womenfolk out here. When she told me she'd marry me, why, I was that proud I could 'a busted my shirt. But the drought was bad last year and we made no crop. We was most likely to starve, I reckon. Then one day when I got back from a huntin' trip, she was gone. I had no idea where she went to but I figured things just got too tough for her. Then, the next thing I knowed, I got a letter from her with fifty dollars in it. 'This here money is for next year's crops,' she said. Well, I found out the letter come from Natchitoches, so I went there to find her and I seen you ridin' outa town. When I learnt from the barkeeper that you spent the night with her, I seen red. The only thing I could think of was killin' you." He made a sound that was part cough and part sob. "I can see now what a fool thing that was to do."

"Did you see your wife before you left?" Luke asked.

"Yeah," the farmer said. "I seen her."

"What did she say?"

"She told me she had another fifty dollars and she was fixin' to come back home. She figured we could make it through another year on a hunnert dollars."

"Can you?"

"I reckon so."

"Then why don't you go back to her, take the money, and get on about your business?"

The farmer sighed, then walked over to pick up his rifle. "I reckon maybe I will," he said.

Luke watched him walk away, grateful that the farmer had the courage to meet him face to face, rather than bushwhack him. Shooting from ambush would have been much easier and Luke knew that many who were bent on killing someone would have selected that course. The farmer mounted his horse and rode away without looking back.

As Luke thought back over the encounter, he started to laugh, more from relief than from amusement.

"Calhoun?" someone called as Luke approached the settlement. It was Reuben Butcher, the wagon master: a short, stocky man with snow-white hair and a beard that made him look older than his fifty years.

"Yes?"

"Here it is," Reuben said. He took out five silver dollars and handed them to Luke.

"What's this?"

Reuben chuckled. "I don't wonder you don't remember. You give me seven dollars to hold last night and told me to give you five back this mornin'. That was to keep you from spendin' ever' cent you had."

Luke ran his hand through his hair, which was still wet from his dunking.

"Yeah," he said. "Yeah, I remember now. Thanks, Reuben."

Reuben chuckled again. "Don't thank me. That was the easiest two dollars I ever made. You'll be wantin' somethin' to eat, I reckon. Mrs. Tresler has some beans ready over to the second wagon there."

"Thanks again," Luke said. "That sounds good."

Mrs. Tresler made change from a cigar box wrapped in a quilt. Then she spooned a generous helping of beans into a bowl and handed it to Luke.

"There's hot peppers on the string over there if you're of a mind," she said, pointing to a long string of dark red, purple, and black dried peppers.

Luke picked off a couple of the peppers and ground them over the beans between his thumb and forefinger. He sat down on a boulder and began to eat.

Chapter 2

Caroline Lafont walked along the old road between a canal and the grove of moss-draped oaks that surrounded the deteriorating colonial mansion which was her home. She lived with her mother and two younger sisters on the sugar plantation her father had founded. She, her mother, and her sisters were living alone because Caroline's father had made a business trip to Texas the previous spring. Now, in January of 1836, nearly a year later, Henri Lafont still had not returned and no one had heard from him.

The talk in nearby New Orleans was that some evil must have befallen him. Only a week ago, when she accompanied her mother to a dance recital in the city, Caroline had overheard several other sugar planters talking about her father.

"It ain't like Henri to jes' up and take off like that," one of the men said. "I tell you, somethin' has happened to him."

"Mos' likely what's happened to him, is he's met

up with a little Mexican wench," one of the others said, and he and several others laughed.

"No, not Henri," the first one insisted. "You know he don' even take to the women at LaBelle's. I'm tellin' you, the man is dead!"

"Shush, that's his daughter standin' over there."

"She couldn't 'a heard nothin'," one of the others said confidently.

He was wrong. The men had been standing in the corner of a square of buildings and the adjoining walls produced an acoustical phenomenon that transmitted their voices as clearly as if they had been talking through a speaking horn. Caroline had heard every word very clearly, though she made a great effort not to disclose that fact.

Caroline was worried about her father. It was not like him to stay away so long without sending word to his family. She would rather suffer the disgrace of her father having deserted the family than suffer the grief of some tragedy. Neither possibility was pleasant to think about and yet she had to assume, as did the planters, that her father's silence had to be explained by one of those two hypotheses: desertion or death. That was the logical assumption and, yet, in her heart, Caroline felt that neither explanation was correct. Her father was alive and well, she knew that. And he had not abandoned his family. She knew that also. There was an explanation for his long and mysterious absence. She didn't know what the explanation was, or even why she felt so strongly about it, but she knew it.

Caroline thought of the mystery of her father's continued absence as she walked along the road. She looked down at the canal and saw the water-lily pads floating on its still surface. A great frog sat on one of the pads, looking up at her curiously. On the other side of the canal, rabbits worked through the brambles, and mockingbirds were singing in the trees. The sky was blue and the sun shone warm for a January day. In the distance, Caroline saw a carriage approaching and shielded her eyes to look at it. She recognized it at once and she felt a certain dread.

The carriage belonged to Frank Sweeny, her father's partner in the plantation. He lived in a fine house in New Orleans and managed the business end of the plantation, contracting the sugar and arranging for shipping. He had stopped by the plantation frequently to look after things in Henri's absence.

Caroline didn't like Frank Sweeny. He was in his late forties, overweight, and balding, and Caroline had never seen anyone who perspired so much. He had to wipe his face with a handkerchief, even in the cool days of January, and, within a short while, the handkerchief would be wringing wet. Although she was uneasy around him, she knew that she had to be courteous to him because he was her father's partner.

Caroline started back to the house, cutting across the yard to arrive at the front porch before Frank did. At twenty-one, Caroline was the oldest of three daughters.

Henri had been disappointed that his firstborn child was a girl. As a result, he had raised her just as he would have raised a son and he had been rewarded with a daughter who was strong of body and limb, at home on the back of a horse, and able to hunt and shoot with the best of men.

Marlene Lafont provided Caroline with the proper education for a young lady so that Caroline now possessed the greatest virtues of both parents. From her father, she received strength and spirit, from her mother, a sense of pride in her womanhood and an appreciation of the gentle arts.

"Mr. Sweeny was here three days ago," Marlene said after greeting her daughter, "I can't imagine why he would come again so soon."

"Whatever it is, I wish he had sent word rather than come here."

"Caroline, that kind of remark isn't becoming to a young lady," Marlene corrected.

Caroline walked up the porch steps and stood with her mother, watching, as the carriage turned into the long, curving driveway. Frank Sweeny halted his team in front of the porch, then looked up at the two women. He wiped his forehead and the top of his head with his handkerchief, then he stuffed the handkerchief inside his vest.

"Good afternoon, ladies," he said to them. "I trust ever'one is in good health and spirits?"

"Good afternoon, Mr. Sweeny. Yes, we are doing well, thank you," Marlene said.

"We are as healthy as we were when you inquired about us just three days ago," Caroline added, a bit more testily.

Frank laughed. "Yes, I was just here, wasn't I? But I've come today for a good reason. Not that I don't have a good reason every time I come," Frank said. He picked up a valise from the floor of his carriage, opened it, and pulled out an envelope. "But this time I have a letter from Henri Lafont."

"Oh, Mr. Sweeny! You've heard from Father?" Caroline cried happily. She started down the steps and reached anxiously for the letter.

Frank held the letter out of her reach.

"No, no, my dear," he said. "I'm afraid you don't understand. This letter isn't for you!"

"I don't believe my father would send you a letter and not send one to us," Caroline said.

"He didn't send this letter."

"But you said—"

"I said I have a letter from your father and so I do," Frank replied. "But it isn't a recent letter. It is an old letter from many years ago, a letter written at the time we entered into partnership."

"Mr. Sweeny, why are you bringing us a letter my father wrote over twenty years ago?" Caroline asked. "What does that have to do with us?"

"Oh, it has a great deal to do with you, I'm afraid," Frank said. He cleared his throat. "You see, child, the terms of this letter are identical to the terms of a letter I wrote at that time. In formulating our partnership, Henri Lafont promised that, should anything happen to him, all of his holdings would come to me. And, of course, I made the same arrangement with him."

"Mr. Sweeny, I still don't understand what you're trying to tell me," Caroline said, though a sickening, sinking sensation in her stomach warned her of the possible consequences of such a letter.

"It's quite simple, really," Frank Sweeny said. "This letter states that, in the event of your father's death, I inherit everything he owns."

"But what about us?" Caroline asked. "What about

my mother and my sisters and me? Are you telling me that we stand to inherit nothing?"

"I'm afraid that is true, my dear," Frank said.

"Well, no matter. When Father gets back, I shall have him change the letter."

"Ah, if only it were that simple for you, my dear," Frank said. "Unfortunately, I now have reason to believe your father is dead. I believe he perished in Texas. Therefore, I have no recourse but to exercise the option afforded me by this letter."

"Mr. Sweeny, have you heard some news about my husband?" Marlene asked. It was the first time she had spoken since Frank produced the letter.

"No," Frank replied. "Nothing specific, that is. I have heard rumors of the death of a tall Louisiana planter though and that can only be Henri."

"Rumors are not fact, Mr. Sweeny," Marlene said in a calm, controlled voice. "Until I hear facts, I shall not consider my Henri dead."

"Yes, well, you must consider my position, Mrs. Lafont. A great deal of money stands to change hands, once Henri's death is certified. Therefore, I have gone to the court and the judge has issued a writ stating that, unless Henri Lafont shows himself to be alive within the next six months, he shall be declared legally dead and all his property and holdings shall be turned over to me."

"But you can't do that!" Caroline said. "You can't get a judge to say my father is dead if he *isn't* dead."

"Oh, but I can," Frank said. "I'm sure you will agree with me that six months is ample time for Henri to prove himself alive…if he is alive."

"But he may not hear about this limitation the

judge has placed on him. He could be incorrectly declared dead by default," Caroline complained.

"In the world of business, my dear, it is all the same thing," Frank said. "If the judge isn't satisfied that your father is alive by July fourth, all his holdings become my property."

"But my mother—my sisters!" Caroline said. "What's going to happen to them?"

Frank chuckled but Caroline heard very little humor in his laugh. He wiped his face with his handkerchief again.

"I find it interesting that you haven't inquired as to your *own* fate," he said.

"For myself, I am not worried," Caroline said.

"Nor should you be," Frank said. "You see, my dear, I have plans for you. Wonderful plans that will solve everything for all of us."

"What are you talking about?"

"My dear, for all your innocence, it cannot have escaped your attention that I am interested in you. I have long wanted you for my own." Frank wiped his face again and cleared his throat. "Therefore, it is with a great deal of pleasure that I offer you a solution to your dilemma. And, of course, when I say *you*, I mean your mother and sisters as well."

Frank was smiling at Caroline now and his smile unnerved her. It gave her a queasy feeling as if she had just taken a dose of castor oil. She didn't want to hear his solution. She didn't even want to listen to his voice. But she knew that she owed that much to her mother and sisters.

"What ..." she started, then she stopped and drew a

deep breath before she spoke again. "What is your 'solution'?" she finally asked.

"It's quite simple," he said. "You can save this plantation by marrying me."

"You are asking me to marry you?"

"Yes, and I would be exceedingly callous to turn out my own wife and her family now, wouldn't I?"

"Mr. Sweeny, I..." Caroline paused in midsentence. She had been about to tell him that she would never marry him. And, for herself, she never would. But she had her mother and sisters to think of. What sort of life would they lead if they were all turned out of their home? She sighed, then looked down at the steps. "I'll think about it," she said quietly.

"Well, don't think too long," Frank said. "I've been patient for a long time. I don't know how much longer I can wait."

"I'll let you know soon," she said.

Caroline felt so weak that she had to hold on to one of the columns that supported the portico roof. She stood quietly with her mother, as Frank snapped the reins at his team, then drove away.

"Caroline," Marlene said when Frank was out of hearing, "you can't mean you would seriously consider that man's offer?"

"I—I didn't know what else to do," Caroline answered. "I couldn't bear to see you and Joelle and Bettina turned out."

"We've got six months before that is supposed to happen," Marlene said. "We can pray diligently at every mass that your father will return home before then."

Joelle and Bettina had been at their lessons and

were just now returning. Bettina, the ten-year-old, was skipping along gaily, while Joelle, two years older, tried to exhibit a decorum suitable to her advanced age as she walked up the drive.

"Mother, let's not tell them," Caroline said. "I'd rather spare them this."

"Yes, I agree," Marlene said. She sighed. "It is so unlike your father not to write. Perhaps—perhaps Mr. Sweeny is right. Maybe he is—"

"No," Caroline interrupted. "Father is not dead! I know it. I can feel it inside. He is *not* dead!"

"Perhaps you are right," Marlene said. "And yet if we have no such proof within six months, it will make no difference."

"Mother, suppose we *did* have proof?" Caroline suggested. "Even if father wasn't here, if we had proof he was still alive, would we still lose the plantation?"

"If we had proof, we could stay here. I'm sure of it," Marlene said.

"Then we'll pray at mass as you suggested," Caroline said. "But I shall do more."

"What do you mean?"

"I'm going to Texas to find him," Caroline said.

Marlene gasped and put her hand on her daughter's arm. "Caroline, no," she said. "You can't do that."

"Why not?"

"Because it is much too arduous and dangerous a journey for a young girl."

"Mother I am not a young girl. I am a woman. I am not a weak woman, either, as you and father have both observed."

"But you don't know where Henri is. You don't know where to start looking for him."

"He's somewhere in Texas."

"Somewhere in Texas? Caroline, you have heard of Texas. It is as big as the rest of Mexico. It is nearly as big as all the states in America!"

"I don't care if it is as big as the entire North American continent," Caroline said. "I am *going* to find my father."

Marlene looked at her daughter for a long moment. Then, when she was convinced that no further pleas on her part would dissuade her, she put her arms out and pulled Caroline to her.

"Oh, please, my darling, do take care," she said. "I can't bear to think of anything happening to you."

"I will be very careful, Mother," Caroline said.

"When are you going?"

"I'll leave tomorrow," Caroline said. "Mother, I'll need the best horse we have. I shall have to take Diablo."

"Yes, dear I understand," Marlene said.

"Why are you hugging Caroline?" Bettina asked as the two younger girls reached the porch.

"Because she's my little girl," Marlene said brightly, trying to hide the tears that had formed in her eyes. "Can't I hug my little girl any time I want to?"

"Caroline's not a little girl, she's a big girl," Bettina said. "I'm a little girl."

"Why, then, I suppose I should hug you too, shouldn't I?" Marlene said. She hugged Bettina and Joelle for a long moment, putting all the anguish and the fear and the love she felt in that one embrace. Finally, she told the two girls that there were some freshly baked sweetmeats in the kitchen and both girls hurried away for their after-school treat.

"Come with me for a moment," Marlene said, mysteriously. She motioned to Caroline.

Caroline followed her mother inside the house, up the wide, sweeping staircase, and into her mother's room. Marlene lifted the seat cushion from one of the chairs in the bedroom, then slid a small wooden panel to one side, exposing a false bottom to the chair. From the secret hiding place, she took a little sack.

"I have three hundred dollars here," she said.

"Mother that's a fortune!" Caroline gasped. "How did you come by so much money?"

"It was my dowry," Marlene said. "My father sent me to your father with three hundred dollars in gold. Henri has never let me touch any of it. Now, I want you to have it."

"No, I can't take it," Caroline said. "You will need it."

"We'll get by," Marlene said. "It's you I'm worried about. You can't make such a long journey with no money at all."

"No," Caroline said again, "I won't take it."

Marlene sighed. "Caroline, I know you are headstrong enough to go on this journey even without my blessing. But wouldn't you rather go *with* it?"

"Yes, of course."

"Then take the money. If you refuse it, I will not allow you to leave."

"I'll take half of it," Caroline finally agreed.

Marlene smiled. "All right," she said as she reached into the sack. "I will feel better knowing that you have some money. Now, we must find some way to hide it, so you won't be a tempting target for road agents. I know...we'll sew the coins into your petticoats. Not all of them in one petticoat, of course, for it would be too heavy. We'll spread the gold out, one or two coins in each petticoat you take."

Caroline laughed. "I'm not going to take any petticoats," she said. "I'm going to Texas, not to a dance."

"Perhaps so," Marlene answered. "But even in Texas, I expect you to dress and act like a lady."

"That's just what I cannot do," Caroline said. "Mother, I shall take one of Father's saddles and I'll dress like a man."

"What?" Marlene asked, scandalized by her daughter's announcement.

"I have to dress like a man, don't you understand? In the first place, men's clothing is much better suited to long journeys than women's clothing is. I also think I will be safer if people think I'm a man. One man traveling alone will not attract the attention one woman would."

Marlene sighed and then reluctantly agreed. "You're right, of course. Come, we have a busy night ahead of us. We must alter your father's clothes to fit you. I'll sew the gold coins in the vest."

Caroline hugged her mother "Thank you," she said, her eyes brimming with tears. "No daughter ever had a finer mother than you."

Caroline and her mother worked until quite late, altering trousers, shirts, a jacket, and a vest. They finished just before midnight. Then, exhausted by her labors, but excited about her plans, Caroline went to bed. The next day, she would begin a new life.

Chapter 3

Caroline had avoided people as much as possible during her ride so far. When she did find it necessary to communicate with others, she told them her name was Carl. So far, no one had guessed her secret.

Only the day before, she had heard of the settlement and the wagon train going west. She'd hurried here from the Louisiana side of the river, hoping to join the wagon train, thinking that it would be a safer and more certain way of getting to Texas to find her father. She had been disappointed when she learned that the wagon train would have to wait for more members. That very afternoon, however, five more wagons arrived. With eleven wagons, the wagon master might feel it was safe to go on.

Reuben Butcher called a meeting of everyone associated with the wagons and Caroline attended. Still dressed as a man, she leaned against a nearby willow tree, watching and listening.

"I say we go on," one of the men said. "I want to get settled into my place soon as I can."

"Settled into your place? How do you know you even have a place?" another asked.

"Because I've got it bought and paid for, that's how I know," the man replied. "And, I've got the deed in my pocket."

"If the Mexicans win this war that deed ain't worth the paper it's printed on," the second man scoffed.

"I'd like to see a bunch of Mexicans run me off my land," the first man challenged belligerently.

"Look, worryin' about the Mexicans runnin' us off our land is just the half of it," another said. "They's a chance we won't even get through if we go now. Iffen we was to meet up with Santa Anna's army, why, they'd wipe us out like they was steppin' on a bunch of ants."

Luke had been standing in front of Lightfoot's tent listening idly to the discussion.

"Let me ask Mr. Calhoun there what he thinks," Reuben said, pointing to Luke. "Luke, you think we should go on?"

One of the settlers spoke before Luke could reply. "Wait a minute before we get his opinion on this. Has he got a wagon in this train?"

"No, he hasn't," Reuben said. "But I'd like to hear what he has to say."

"Ain't he the fella that got into a fight this mornin' over another man's wife?"

"Yeah, that's him," another said.

"And I seen him so drunk last night he could scarcely stand," another put in.

"Drinkin' *and* fightin', was he? Don't seem to me

like a fella of his low character got much right to say nothin' 'bout our business."

"That's where you're wrong," Reuben said. "I've already asked Luke Calhoun to serve as chief scout and hunter for us. When we leave here, he'll be goin' with us."

"I don't want the likes of him aroun' my wife," one of the men said.

"Do you all feel that way?" Reuben asked. "Because I tell you now and I tell you true, iffen Luke Calhoun don't go with this train, then I don't intend to lead it."

"Story I got is that fella's wife was workin' as a saloon girl over in Natchitoches," someone said.

"Seems to me like any honest wife would be safe around Calhoun. I ain't got no qualms," another man said.

"I reckon our women'd be safe enough from him," another put in. "I got no quarrel with his goin'." Caroline looked more closely at the man called Luke Calhoun as the discussion continued. She had a strong sense of curiosity about him and wondered what sort of trouble he'd had over the saloon girl. Then, she realized exactly what sort of trouble they were talking about and, inexplicably, she blushed at her thoughts and looked down at the ground quickly, hoping no one had noticed. A girlish blush could cause people to suspect she was a woman.

"Mr. Calhoun, do you feel we'd be safe from Santa Anna?"

"From Santa Anna, yes, you are safe," Luke said. "He may stop you, he may turn you around and send you back, but he won't use more force than is necessary and he won't rob you. There are others, though, who aren't as gentlemanly as Santa Anna and his officers."

"What others are you talking about?"

"Renegades," Luke said. "Deserters who have formed roving outlaw bands and who are totally without honor."

"I ain't likely to be put to fear by no bunch of Mexican deserters," one of the men scoffed.

"Not just Mexicans," Luke said. "There are some Texans and Americans as well. Mexico doesn't have a lock on desperadoes."

"It don't make me no never mind. We can handle near anythin' that comes up, iffen we stick together. I say let's go."

"That's big talk from you, Moultin. You got no one but yourself," one of the others said to the bold speaker, "They's some of us here got families, ol' folks, and little children to think of besides ourselves. I'm not goin'."

"I'm not goin' either," another man put in.

"Well, if they don' go, then I sure ain't gonna go either," a third man said. "That would cut our strength down to nine wagons. I don't think that's enough to get us to Texas safely."

"If you don't go, that cuts it down to eight and I'm not going to try it with eight," another man said.

"Well, then, there you have it," Reuben said, closing the meeting. "We ain't goin' till some more wagons show up."

"When will that be?" someone called.

"Last month, I heered of the Perkins party formin' a train. Anyone else heered of 'em?" another asked.

"Yeah, they got ten wagons."

"All right," Reuben said. "Most likely, they'll be here within the month. At that time, we'll have enough wagons to go anywhere we want. Until then, my advice to ever'one is just to sit tight here in camp. Make sure your wagons is in good repair and your stock is healthy. Get lots of rest. You're gonna need it."

———

CAROLINE WAS DISAPPOINTED that the wagon train wasn't going on. She wished desperately to continue her journey for she had to find her father quickly if she wanted to save the Lafont home.

Well, that wouldn't stop her. If the wagon train insisted on staying here, she would go on alone.

The man called Luke Calhoun walked over to a water barrel and scooped out a drink. Caroline watched him silently. Perhaps she could hire him to take her to Texas. After all, the wagon train had voted not to go on, so he was without a job.

Caroline walked over to Luke Calhoun and watched him as he drank. He took long gulps and then carefully hung the dipper on the rim of the barrel. He wiped his chin with the back of his hand and looked at Caroline. He had the most penetrating eyes she had ever seen. He scooped up a dipperful of water and handed it to Caroline. As yet, neither of them had spoken, though their eyes had taken each other's measure.

"Thank you," Caroline said, surprised by his action. She took a drink, then looked down to avoid his unwavering gaze. Finally, she finished the water and handed him the dipper "Mr. Calhoun? Is that your name?"

"Yes," Luke said.

"I am Carl Lafont. I wish to speak with you about employment."

"I'm not hiring anyone," Luke answered.

Caroline laughed. "No, you don't understand," she said. "I'm not seeking employment. I would like you to work for me."

"Doing what?" Luke said.

"I want you to help me find my father," Caroline said.

"Where is he?"

"In Texas."

"Texas is a big place. That doesn't tell me anything."

"I'm sorry," Caroline said. "That's all I can say because I don't know exactly where he is. I only know that he is my father and I miss him and…and a great deal of wealth is at stake. I *must* find him."

"I see," Luke said. "And what, exactly, would you have me do?"

"I will need the services of a skilled scout and hunter like you if my search is to be successful."

"I'm not interested," Luke said.

"What? But wait a minute. We haven't even discussed it yet. I'm prepared to pay you handsomely for your services."

"Nothing to discuss," Luke said. "I'm not taking you."

"But why? Give me one good reason why you won't help me.

"Texas is too dangerous a place, right now, for a young woman traveling alone," Luke said.

Caroline gasped. "How did you know?"

"I know," Luke said.

"But you do claim to be a guide and hunter?"

"Yes."

"Then why won't you let me hire you?"

"Because I've no mind to lead a beautiful young woman to her death," Luke said.

"Surely you are exaggerating the danger?"

"Tell me, Miss Lafont, why is it so important that you find your father?"

"I must prove that he is still alive," Caroline said. "An unscrupulous man named Frank Sweeny is my father's business partner. He has filed a claim against our property based on an old agreement between him and my father. If I cannot prove that my father is alive, then Mr. Sweeny will take everything."

"Surely you can reason with him?" Luke suggested.

"I wish I could," Caroline said. "Unfortunately, he is not a reasonable man. He has stated that he intends to take possession of our land. The only way out would be for me to—" Caroline stopped in midsentence, just letting her words hang.

"For you to what?" Luke asked.

"For me to marry him," Caroline said, speaking so quietly that the words could scarcely be heard.

Luke laughed. "Well, there you have your solution. All you have to do is marry him."

"I could never marry him," Caroline spat. "Never! Not in a hundred years!"

"Why not, if it would save your land?"

"Because I don't love him," Caroline said.

"What difference does that make? Many women marry men they don't love."

"I will marry *only* for love," Caroline said resolutely.

Luke looked at her and though the laughter had left his lips, it hadn't left his eyes. "Yes," Luke finally managed to say. "Marry for love ... by all means. But, Miss Lafont, if you are to live long enough to find the man you love, then I suggest you turn around and go back home. As I explained to you, Texas is no place for you now."

She had to get to Texas. She had to find her father with or without this man's help.

"Very well," she said. "I have come this far alone. I'll go the rest of the way alone."

Luke laughed. "You have come this far? From where, New Orleans? That is but a short distance over well-traveled roads. There are settlements along the way and farms and plantations. Most of the people you met along the way were peaceful folk, civilized by gentle upbringing. You have not been in danger until this point but you can't go any farther without putting yourself in serious danger. I say you *can't* go on."

"And I say you have no authority over me," Caroline said hotly. "I am going on, sir. I *am* going on, whether you like it or not!"

Luke looked at her for a moment longer then let his breath out in one long sigh.

"Look, wait a short while. More wagons will arrive soon and the train will go on then. I'll scout for the wagon train then and I'll look out for you."

"You'll look out for me? Mr. Calhoun, for your

information, I neither want nor need your protection. If you will consent to guide me into Texas, I will follow your instructions to the letter. But if your only connection with me is to be in your capacity as scout for a wagon train, then I want none of it."

"I'm trying to help you," Luke said.

"If you really want to help, take me to Texas. We can leave now, today. Every moment I stay here is a moment wasted."

"Try to understand, Miss Lafont. There is a war going on in Texas."

"There have been wars before," Caroline said.

"Not like this one," Luke said. "This war is unique because there is no right—only wrong. On the one hand, we have robbers, on the other, thieves. You won't be safe, no matter where you are."

"I'm prepared to take that risk."

"You'll take it without me," Luke said.

Luke turned and walked away and Caroline watched him with a sinking heart. He wasn't going to take her but that didn't mean she wasn't going to go. It would have been so much simpler, though, if he had agreed to go with her. Caroline looked around at the wagons, silently cursing the fear that kept the train from leaving. She saw a table set up in front of one wagon and she realized that the owners of that wagon were selling some of their possessions. Among the goods for sale was a pretty calico dress.

Caroline got an idea.

By nightfall, a dozen campfires were burning and several settlers had begun to dance to the music of a fiddle, a jug, a Jew's harp, and a washboard. Caroline looked through the crowd until she spotted Luke

Calhoun leaning against the tongue of a wagon, watching the merriment. She walked over and stood quietly behind him, just looking at the back of his neck. Finally, he felt the heat of her stare and turned.

"Well," he said, appreciatively, "I must say, I prefer you dressed this way."

Caroline was wearing the calico dress and now she knew she had made the right decision. The dress had its desired effect: Luke Calhoun was very much aware of her as a woman. But then, so would anyone be, for the dress molded itself to her curves and she was a picture of feminine grace and beauty.

"Do you like it?" she asked.

"Yes," Luke said. "I like it a great deal."

"Enough to ask me to dance?" Caroline said brazenly. Luke smiled broadly and reached for her hand to lead her to the circle of dancers.

Caroline loved to dance. She had attended many cotillions in New Orleans and once was mentioned in the *Picayune* as the most graceful dancer in all of Louisiana. She was pleased to note that, despite his great size, Luke Calhoun was light on his feet. They made a striking pair: he big and handsome, she graceful and pretty.

The others noticed the couple immediately. Although most of them had seen Caroline before, they didn't realize it, for she had been disguised as a boy.

"Who's the girl with Calhoun?" they whispered. "Where did she come from?"

"I don't know but, if they's a pretty girl anywhere abouts, you can count on Calhoun to find her," another said.

Caroline danced every dance with Luke Calhoun.

Finally, when both of them were very warm and breathing heavily, Luke said, "Come, we'll walk down to the river. The breeze off the water will be cool."

Caroline walked with Luke, leaving the music and the dancers behind them. Soon, the laughter seemed as distant as a memory. Like the memory of her father.

Caroline plucked a wildflower. In the moonlight, its colors were muted, though she could still smell its fragrance. Crickets chirped and frogs called.

"I'm glad you've reconsidered," Luke said.

"What are you talking about? I haven't reconsidered anything," Caroline said.

"But I thought—" Luke began. "I mean, you're wearing a dress instead of men's clothes. Surely you mean to go back home."

"No, Mr. Calhoun," Caroline said. "I'm going on to Texas. I mean to try one last time to talk you into going with me."

"All your wiles won't get you anything from me. I will not take you to Texas—and that is final!"

Caroline whirled angrily and walked away.

Chapter 4

Having revealed herself as a woman, Caroline deemed it no longer prudent to disguise herself as a man. Wearing the calico dress, she went through the encampment until she found a Mexican guide who was willing to take her to Texas. That settled, she sold Diablo and bought a horse and carriage.

The entire encampment knew of her intention to proceed on into Texas. Some tried to warn her against it, while others were open in their admiration. Those who had voted to go on held her up as an example to the others and some even considered going with her. She knew that their lumbering wagons would have slowed her down, though, and she was glad when they decided to stay where they were.

Caroline's carriage was waiting in front of Lightfoot's tent while the Mexican guide filled the water barrel from the river. Caroline was sitting in the back seat when Luke walked up to her.

"You are still going through with this foolish adventure of yours?" Luke asked.

"I intend to find my father," Caroline answered. She brushed an imaginary piece of lint from her skirt. One might have thought she was going for a leisurely ride down Canal Street in New Orleans rather than beginning a thousand-mile foray into war-torn Texas.

"I hoped you would go back home when I refused to guide you."

"As you can see, I hired another guide."

"He should have turned you away, too. But then Gonzara never could turn his back on a woman."

"Unlike you."

"Unlike me…though the time will come when you will wish that Gonzara had done just as I did."

"Why do you say that? Have I something to fear from my guide?"

Luke chuckled.

"No, you've nothing to fear from Gonzara. He is a decent enough man and he will serve you as faithfully as he can. It is just that he will be limited in what he can do. Just as I would be. The only difference is that I am willing to admit to my limitations."

Gonzara returned to the carriage then, groaning under the load of the full water cask. He set it in the bed of the carriage, then wiped the sweat from his brow and gave Luke a wide grin.

"Good morning, Senor Calhoun," Gonzara said. He nodded toward Caroline. "I have with me one *muy bonita señorita*, eh?"

"Yes, Gonzara," Luke said. "Why are you taking her?"

"Why? Because, she must find her father, *senor*. Has she not told you her story?"

"She told me."

"And you would not help her?" Gonzara said. He clucked his tongue and wagged his head disapprovingly. "Senor Calhoun, I did not think you could deny to help someone in such need."

"Gonzara, you know damn well Texas is crawling with scum who'd give anything to have such a woman. Do you really intend to expose her to such danger?"

"I can avoid the soldiers," Gonzara said. "I know a secret way."

A few minutes later, the carriage drove out through a road that had been cut through the canebrake and the encampment disappeared from view. Caroline settled into her seat for the long ride.

As the hours passed, she weighed the advantages and disadvantages of having bought the carriage. Its padded seat was definitely more comfortable than Diablo's back and she could doze while Gonzara did the driving. That was the advantage. The disadvantage was the slowness of the vehicle. Alone, on horseback, she could have traveled twice as fast.

Of course, if she had gone on alone, she would probably have lost her way, whereas Gonzara seemed to know exactly where he was headed. Caroline found that very reassuring.

They rode all that day and Caroline looked out over the vast land they were passing through. She could clearly see the attraction such a place had for so many people. Here was wonderful land, stretching for as far as the eye could see, and there was no one here.

They made camp just after sundown. Gonzara laid

a blanket out next to the fire for Caroline, then moved several feet away to spread his bedroll.

Though Caroline had dozed fitfully during the day, she slept soundly that night and didn't awaken until a delightful aroma assailed her nostrils the next morning. She opened her eyes and saw Gonzara bending over a pot of fresh coffee which he had suspended from a crosspiece over the fire.

"Ah, you are awake," Gonzara said. He poured some coffee into a tin cup and handed it to Caroline. The cup was hot and Caroline set it down quickly.

"*Gracias,*" Caroline said.

Gonzara poured his own coffee and blew into the cup to cool the scalding drink. Caroline wondered how he could stand to hold the cup.

Gonzara was in his late thirties, short, heavy-set, and with his dark hair, laced with gray. Caroline had found him to be a quiet, pleasant man.

"Ah, *señorita,*" Gonzara said, "why do men go to war anywhere? Because they do not follow God's law and because there is much greed among them."

"Is greed what causes this war?"

"*Sí.*"

"Greed on the part of the Mexicans or the Texans?"

"There are no Texans, *señorita.*" Gonzara said. "There are only Americans who have come to Texas."

"Then you are saying that the war is the fault of the Americans?"

"No," Gonzara said. "Many of the Americans have come to Texas legally. They have bought land and they wish only to settle down and farm their acreage."

"What is wrong with that?" Caroline asked.

"There is nothing wrong with that. That is a noble ambition. But the Mexicans will not let them do it."

"Why not?"

"Some Mexicans fear that too many Americans will take away power from them. Others feel that the Spanish land grant authorities had no right to sell land to the Americans. There is much hate between the two sides."

"Do you hate the Americans?" Caroline asked.

"I hate no one, *señorita*, except those who give me reason to hate them."

Caroline reached for her coffee cup, found it cool enough to touch, and drank it, gratefully.

Over the next two days, she discovered, to her surprise, that Gonzara was from one of the wealthiest families in Mexico. Some months before, he had compromised a young woman from another prominent family. As a result of his indiscretion, Gonzara had gone into exile.

On the third day of their journey, they came to a farmhouse. Caroline was eager to talk to someone other than Gonzara and she smiled as they approached the house.

Evidently, her company was just as eagerly sought, for the husband and wife and four young children turned out to greet them as they approached the house.

"Welcome, welcome!" the man called. "Come inside and rest, drink some water and stay for supper!"

"Thank you," Caroline said, stepping down from the carriage gingerly, then stretching her aching muscles.

"*Señor,* may I tend to the horse?" Gonzara asked.

"Of course," the man agreed. "Come with me." Caroline went inside the house at the woman's insistence. She sank down on the sofa and gratefully accepted a glass of cool water.

"It comes from our well," the woman said. "It's the best tasting water in the world."

Caroline drank it appreciatively. It did taste much better than the slightly rank water from the barrel she and Gonzara were carrying.

Caroline looked around the rustic house. It was unpainted and the boards were loosely fitted together as if the house had been built by one man, working alone. Despite that, there was a charm, almost a beauty to the place, and Caroline could see that the woman was very proud of it.

"You have a nice home," Caroline said.

The woman smiled broadly. "When Mr. Sullivan, my husband, asked me to come out here with him, I told him that I wouldn't leave Missouri unless he could promise me a house just like the one we were living in there. He agreed and, well, here we are."

"You are farming here now?"

"Yep. More'n fifteen hundred acres," the woman said proudly.

"My! What are you growing on a farm so large?"

"Kids, mostly," Mrs. Sullivan replied with a laugh. She pointed to the four youngsters of various ages who were looking on in undisguised fascination. Caroline assumed they were interested in her because she was a visitor, a somewhat rare treat in this area.

"Please stay here with us tonight," Mrs. Sullivan said. "Your driver can sleep in the barn. There is no bed for him but the hay is soft and it is certain to be more comfortable than sleeping on the ground."

"Yes," Caroline said. "You are most kind, Mrs. Sullivan."

"Please call me Lydia," the woman said. "My husband's name is George and we are so happy to have visitors that we will do anything to keep you with us for a while."

Mrs. Sullivan prepared a supper that was bounteous enough for a Christmas feast—fried and baked chicken, an assortment of vegetables, freshly baked bread, a pie, and a cake. The meal was a happy occasion and Caroline was pleased that Gonzara was also welcomed at the table.

"Senor Gonzara has been most gracious during our journey together," she said when she and Mrs. Sullivan were alone together "But he is Mexican and I feared that there would be some difficulty because of the war between his people and ours. I am glad that you made him feel so welcome."

"Well, my dear," Lydia said, "we are all God's children. I don't want my youngsters fighting amongst themselves and I can't see as how the Lord would like fighting any more than I do. I don't know anything about that war. It hasn't reached us yet, and I hope it never does. I don't understand wars at all—especially wars against people I like. And I like nearly all the Mexicans I've ever known."

"*Gracias* for your kindness," Gonzara said, coming back into the room as the woman finished speaking. He pointed to a guitar that was standing in the corner. "Does someone play?"

Dan chuckled. "A fella come through here 'bout a

year ago. He was carryin' the guitar on his saddle and he asked if he could leave it with us. He was afraid it'd get broke if he carried it with him. I told him I'd look out for it and it's been sittin' there in the corner ever since."

Gonzara walked over to the instrument and picked it up, gently, lovingly.

"This is a very fine guitar," he said. "I understand why the man did not wish to take it with him."

Gonzara strummed it, saw that it was out of tune, then he began to tune the strings.

"Do you play that thing?" George asked.

"Yes," Gonzara said.

"Play somethin' for us."

"I don't know, it is not my guitar."

"Senor Gonzara, please play for us," Caroline said. "It's the least we can do to repay the Thompsons for their hospitality."

Gonzara smiled. "How can I resist the request of one so beautiful?" he said.

Gonzara played several chords, then stopped. Caroline started to ask him what was wrong. Then she saw that he was bowing his head, almost as if in prayer. Was he praying? If so, for what? That he would play well? The expression on his face when he picked up the guitar was one of such joy that she thought he had said a prayer of thanks for the opportunity to play again.

After a few more seconds of silence, Gonzara began to play. The music spilled out, a steady, unwavering beat with two or three poignant minor chords at the end of phrases but with an overall, single-string melody weaving in and out among the chords like a thread of gold woven through the finest cloth.

The music spoke of joy and sorrow, pain and pleasure. It moved into Caroline's soul and she found herself being carried along with the melody, now rising, now falling. Perhaps it was the moment, the quiet, the softly lit room, the weight of her personal sorrows, but Caroline had never before been so deeply moved by music. She sat spellbound for several seconds after the last exquisite chord had faded away. Then, when Gonzara, at last, put the instrument down, she began to applaud enthusiastically.

"Bravo, Senor Gonzara, bravo!" she said. "That was wonderful!"

"Yes," Lydia Sullivan agreed, "it truly was."

After supper, George and Gonzara sat on the front porch drinking Sullivan's home-brewed liquor. Caroline helped her hostess wash the dishes and get the children ready for bed. They went most reluctantly because they were still excited over their visitor. She had to promise each of them that she wouldn't leave without saying goodbye.

"You'll have to forgive them," Lydia said when she and Caroline finally sat down. "They are wild with excitement because you are here."

"I have two younger sisters," Caroline said, laughing. "I remember when they were that age. They were the same way."

"Where are they now?"

"They are home in Louisiana with my mother."

"It's none of my business, my dear and you can tell me so if you are of a mind to, but what are you doing out here all alone? Texas isn't a safe place for a young woman to travel through even in good times. Now, with this war going on, why, it's all the worse."

"I've come in search of my father," Caroline said. "I must find him or my mother and my sisters will be turned out of their home."

"Turned out of *their* home? Isn't it *your* home as well?"

"Yes, of course," Caroline said, "but the prospect of being turned out doesn't seem so frightening to me, not now. I just can't bear for it to happen to my mother and the girls."

"Why must you find your father to prevent that?"

Caroline told her the entire story, including Frank Sweeny's offer of marriage. She finished by relating her encounter with Luke Calhoun. "Easily the most unpleasant man I have ever met," she said.

Lydia Sullivan smiled. "Your words say that, Caroline, but your eyes say something else."

"What do you mean?"

"I know Luke Calhoun," she replied. "And I know that if he refused to bring you to Texas, he did so because he thought it would be best for you not to come here. And truth to tell, it probably would have been best. Now, tell me. What is your father's name?"

"Henri," Caroline said. "Some people call him Henry but we pronounce his name the French way. Henri Lafont."

"Henry," Lydia Sullivan said, rubbing her chin. "Henry Lafont. Is he a tall, distinguished-looking gentleman?"

"Yes, yes, that is him," Caroline said. "Oh, Lydia, do you know where he is?"

"I know where he *was* a couple of months ago. He come through here, just like you. He stayed with us for a couple of days."

"Do you know where he is now? Where did he go?"

"He said he was headed for San Antonio," Lydia said.

Caroline and Gonzara left the Sullivan place the next morning after breakfast. Caroline would have left before dawn except for her promise to say good-bye to the children. Also, Lydia clearly wanted them to stay for breakfast to extend the visit and Caroline couldn't disappoint her. Caroline was in high spirits as they left. This was the first news she had had of her father since leaving Louisiana. Surely it would be a simple enough task to go to San Antonio and find him.

"Do you know where San Antonio is?" Caroline asked Gonzara.

"*Sí*," Gonzara said. "I have been there many times."

"Then let's travel as quickly as we can. I want to find my father and take him home with me."

"I will do the best I can, *señorita*." Gonzara said.

"How long will the journey take us?"

"If the weather does not slow us, we should be there within two weeks."

Two weeks! Caroline thought. In but two more weeks she would find her father and this long nightmare would be over.

Would he be well, she wondered? Would he be happy to see her? Would he be surprised? And why had he not written to them? Surely, he would have an explanation.

43

No matter. She would find the answer to all those questions when she saw him again. They would laugh and embrace, and then he would go back home with her, and their plantation would be saved, and she could get back to living a normal life.

Chapter 5

The hot sun and the rocking motion of the carriage lulled Caroline into a light sleep. She thought, later on, that if she had not been dozing, if she had been more alert, she would have seen the riders coming up behind them. Perhaps she could have warned Gonzara. Still, he would have been able to do very little. At least he had died quickly, without ever knowing what had happened.

The shot that killed Gonzara awakened Caroline from her slumber and she screamed. She watched in horror as Gonzara tumbled from the seat, the back of his head red with blood.

The horse bolted and the reins fell out of Caroline's reach so that she had to ride helplessly in the back of the carriage, holding on to the sides.

Riders swooped down on the carriage and quickly moved along both sides. The lead rider grabbed the horse and pulled back on his bridle until the carriage came to a stop. Another dozen riders joined the first one and they all looked down at Caroline. They wore uniforms, of sorts, incomplete and augmented with sombreros and scarves.

They were Mexican.

The riders were talking among themselves in Spanish. Caroline couldn't understand what they were saying but the tone of their voices and the expressions on their faces made it plain that they were discussing things she did not want to hear.

"Who are you?" she asked. "What do you want?"

"Ah, *señorita*, a lady as pretty as you should never ask a man what he wants," one rider said. As he spoke, Caroline saw another rider approach. This one was more elaborately uniformed than the rest with epaulets of gold braid. Caroline guessed that he was the leader.

"Who are you?" Caroline asked.

"Captain Juan Lopez." He removed his hat and bowed gallantly.

Caroline realized that in other circumstances she might have considered him handsome. At the moment, however, his fine-featured face was lost on her.

"Captain Lopez? If you are commissioned, sir, perhaps you are a gentleman."

"Perhaps," he said. "And perhaps, as a *gentleman*, I should apologize for the rude suggestions made by my men though, if you do not speak Spanish, you didn't understand them."

"I speak no Spanish," Caroline said.

"That is good, *señorita*. Their suggestions were quite bold. But of course, you must forgive them. They are convict soldiers, you see."

"What are convict soldiers?" Caroline asked in a frightened tone.

"These men are the scum of the earth. They are here, not out of patriotism, but because the army is an alternative to prison. They have all been convicted of crimes—robbery, murder, rape."

Caroline gasped.

"Do not worry, my pretty one. If you will put yourself in my hands, I will personally guarantee your safety."

"Thank you, Captain Lopez," Caroline said. She turned and looked behind her. She saw Gonzara's body lying in the road, unmoving.

"Gonzara is dead, I'm afraid," Juan Lopez said. "I am sorry my men killed him. He and I were cousins. As children, we played together."

"You killed your own cousin?" Caroline gasped.

"No, not I," Lopez said. "It was one of my men."

"But you are their commanding officer. You are responsible for what they do."

"In an ordinary army, *señorita*, under ordinary circumstances, that would be quite true. But my men are not ordinary soldiers and these are extraordinary circumstances. The rules of conventional warfare and gentlemanly behavior have been suspended, not only by my side, but by yours as well."

"I don't have a side in this war," Caroline said. "I only hope to find my father so that we may return to Louisiana. You can have Texas for all I care."

Lopez laughed. "It is too bad, *señorita*, that you cannot extend your generous offer of Texas in the name of your American criminals, Sam Houston,

Stephen Austin, Davy Crockett, and the murderer from your own state, Jim Bowie."

"Jim Bowie! Is Jim Bowie in Texas?"

"Ah, you know him?"

"My father knows him," Caroline said. "Perhaps my father is *with* him. Tell me, do you know where Jim Bowie is?"

"No. But if your father is with him, then your father is with the rebels."

"Surely not," Caroline said. "Why would my father fight in a war that is none of his concern?"

"Indeed, one might ask Jim Bowie the same question." Lopez said something in Spanish then and one of the soldiers dismounted and climbed into the driver's seat of the carriage.

"I have ordered him to drive you to our headquarters," Lopez explained.

"What will happen to me there?" Caroline asked.

"That all depends upon you, *señorita*."

"How?"

"If you cooperate with me, I promise that you will be released unharmed. If you don't cooperate with me, then perhaps I shall let my soldiers have their way with you." Cold fear swept through Caroline but she said nothing. "I take your silence to mean that you will cooperate with me." Lopez's dark eyes flashed brilliantly, as if from some inner light, and he smiled, his white teeth gleaming against his dark face.

"Ah, wonderful," he said. "Wonderful."

He signaled and his men began to move. They rode fast and the driver of the carriage lashed the horse, trying to force him to keep pace with the others. Soon the horse was covered with foam and Caroline begged the driver to be easy with the poor animal but the soldier understood no English and disregarded her desperate gestures.

Finally, they came to a stream and Caroline caught sight of a cabin and a cluster of tents on the far side. The carriage plunged through the shallow river behind the horsemen, throwing water and sand over Caroline's face and clothing. The men reined in their mounts when they reached the opposite bank.

Lopez swung down from his horse and walked over to the carriage. He offered his hand to help Caroline down. Stiff and aching from the hard ride, she accepted his help. She needed to walk around and stretch her muscles a bit. "What is this place?" she asked.

"The cabin once belonged to a gringo family," Lopez said. "I now use it as my headquarters."

"Where are the people who used to live here?"

"Dead, *señorita*," Lopez said easily. Caroline looked at him sharply. "But we didn't kill them," he added. "They were killed by desperadoes who are without honor and without a flag. Such men fight only for profit."

"And you are *with* honor?" Caroline asked.

"*Señorita*, I, at least, fight under my country's flag," Lopez said. "Are you hungry? We will eat and talk."

Caroline hadn't eaten since early morning and the prospect of a meal sounded good to her. Lopez led her behind the house to the back yard where a Mexican woman was cooking over a wood fire. The pungent aromas of the food assailed Caroline's senses, making her realize how very hungry she was.

"Do you wish to rest, *señorita?* There is a hammock

under the two shade trees beside the hacienda," Lopez offered.

Caroline was too frightened to rest but she hoped that if she accepted his offer she would at least be out of sight of the other soldiers. She thanked Lopez and walked toward the hammock.

"Who is the woman who cooks for you?" she asked.

"Her name is Carmelita," Lopez said. "The men captured her in San Felipe."

"They captured her? But she is Mexican."

"She is also a woman and she serves their needs," Lopez said easily.

"Serves their needs?"

"When the men need a woman, they take Carmelita."

"You mean all of them?" Caroline asked, incredulous.

Lopez chuckled. "Carmelita is an ugly cow, too old to attract men. She pretends that she is held captive against her wishes but when we leave, she does not try to run away. I think she enjoys her position. You should be thankful for her. As long as my men have her to serve them, I can offer you my personal protection."

Caroline shuddered. How awful it would be to be in Carmelita's place! Why didn't the woman attempt to escape?

"If you will excuse me, *señorita*, I will prepare for dinner," Lopez said.

"Do as you wish," Caroline said. "I'm not a guest to whom you must excuse yourself, Captain. I am your prisoner."

"My dear, I only sought to make your time here more comfortable. Forgive me." Lopez touched the brim of his hat in a salute, smiled, and then left.

Caroline sat down in the hammock. She could hear the conversation and the laughter of the men. Though she understood none of what they were saying, she found their laughter unnerving, and she knew they were talking and joking about her. She was glad she couldn't understand them.

After a while, Lopez returned. Caroline nearly didn't recognize him at first. He had bathed and shaved and he was wearing a splendid uniform of green, red, and gold. On his head, he wore a wide-brimmed hat resplendent with feathers and other ornamentation. In a ballroom in New Orleans, the handsome Captain Lopez would have cut such a dashing figure that all the women would have taken their dance cards to him to sign. Here, on the banks of a muddy stream in the wilds of Texas, he looked so incongruous that Caroline felt an irrational urge to laugh but she prudently controlled it.

"Allow me to introduce myself properly, *señorita*," Captain Lopez said. He removed his hat, then made a sweeping, formal bow.

"I am Don Esteban Juan Lopez, formerly a colonel on the personal staff of General Antonio Santa Anna."

"You were on the personal staff of the president of Mexico?" Caroline asked, surprised that he had once held such a high position.

"*Sí, señorita*. With my friend, Major Gonzara."

"I knew that Gonzara was a gentleman," Caroline said. "But he didn't tell me he had served on the general's personal staff. But what happened? Why were the two of you sent here?"

"It is a story heard often, I am sure," Lopez said. "Too much liquor, a pretty girl, and a moment of indiscretion."

"Yes, Gonzara said he had compromised a young lady."

Lopez chuckled. "He was being a loyal officer, even after being cashiered. You see, he was taking the blame for my actions. Of the many indiscretions I have committed, it is ironic that I was to be punished for one for which I had no guilt. I persuaded Gonzara to take the blame because I knew the punishment would be less harsh for him."

Caroline listened in shocked silence.

"You see, *señorita*, for Gonzara the punishment was easy. He was merely discharged from the army and banished from Mexico City. Had I taken complete responsibility, General Santa Anna might have had me shot, even though he knew of my innocence. But, because Gonzara assumed the blame, I was simply demoted and given command of the dregs you see around you." Lopez looked toward the men, one of whom was talking with Carmelita. "Ah," Lopez sighed, "I don't know which of us suffered the greater punishment. To have been reduced from the glory and honor of such a position to this or to have been cashiered."

Caroline's voice was cold and accusing when she spoke. "Gonzara gave up everything for you and you had him killed."

"No, *señorita*, I did not have him killed." Lopez

held up one finger as if explaining something to a child. "One of my men killed him without my knowledge. I didn't even know who the victim was until I saw the body."

"But you showed no remorse, no grief," Caroline said.

"I am a soldier," Lopez replied. "In time of war, I have no time for remorse."

"Couldn't you at least punish the man who killed your friend?"

"But who killed him? And what punishment would you have me mete out?" Lopez smiled. "But enough of this unpleasant talk. Come, there's no elegant ballroom in the cabin but it will be better than eating out here. We shall dine together."

The table in the small house was set with a clean, white cloth and with crockery that Caroline assumed had belonged to the late owners. Her heart sank at the thought of eating off dishes that must have been the pride and joy of a woman who now lay in a shallow grave somewhere nearby. But Caroline knew she would need nourishment and she closed her mind to all other thoughts.

Lopez poured a clear liquid into a glass. "This drink is native to my country," he explained. "It is called Tequila."

Caroline, whose experience with liquor was limited to an occasional glass of wine, looked at the drink uneasily.

"Drink it," Lopez said. "It will make you feel good."

"No."

"Señorita," Lopez said, eyes flashing angrily, "you have a choice. You may drink quietly and willingly with me or I will turn you over to my men and you will drink with them whether you want to or not."

"I will not drink with anyone," Caroline protested.

Lopez leaned toward her menacingly. "Drink," he said.

Caroline, frightened that he would turn her over to his men, picked up the glass and forced the drink down. It burned her throat and she found the taste unpleasant.

Lopez filled the glass a second time.

"Drink!" he ordered again.

Caroline looked at him pleadingly but she saw no compassion in the gaze he returned. She drank the second glass.

The third glass went down more easily, but she felt a spinning lightness in her head.

Time seemed distorted after that. She vaguely remembered eating the meal. Then, the food was gone and Carmelita cleared the table. Candles were lit and Caroline realized that it had grown dark outside.

The tequila loosened her tongue, and she told Lopez of her search for her father, and of her attempt to convince Luke Calhoun to guide her in her search.

"Ah, *señorita,* were I not committed to my duty, I would gladly abandon this command and help you in your search," Lopez said. His statement touched her and she began to think that perhaps he was not as evil as she had feared.

Lopez left, after telling her that she could sleep in the cabin that night. A few moments later, Carmelita came into the room and demanded her clothes.

"What?" Caroline asked, trying hard to focus on what was happening. Her head was spinning so that it was almost impossible. "What are you saying? You want my clothes?"

"*Sí*," Carmelita said. "It is the orders of the captain."

"But why?"

"He is afraid you will run," Carmelita said. "No clothes, no run."

"I most certainly will not take off my clothes," Caroline said. The shocking suggestion had a sobering effect on her.

Carmelita opened the door and two of the convict soldiers stood just on the other side, leering at her.

"The captain said if you no take off your clothes, they will," Carmelita said.

Defeated, Caroline nodded her acquiescence. Carmelita smiled and closed the door shutting the soldiers out of the room.

Caroline took off her dress and handed it to Carmelita.

Carmelita looked at Caroline coldly, dispassionately, then she took the dress and closed the door. Caroline was a prisoner in the wilds of Texas. Despite all that, she was not frightened. Perhaps her fear, like all her other emotions, had been dulled by the drink. Or perhaps she had grown accustomed to danger during the past three weeks. Whatever the reason, she was able to remain calm, and she was proud of that.

Caroline climbed into the bed and covered herself with a patchwork quilt. For an instant, she thought of the hours of work the late owner of this house must have put in on the quilt, but she could not retain the thought. Her head was again spinning from the liquor and the horrible events of the day.

Caroline was surprised at how good it felt to lie down. She had had a terrifying and exhausting day. She closed her eyes and was asleep within moments.

Chapter 6

Caroline was awakened by the sound of shooting outside. The shots were rapid and ear-splitting and she sat up in bed, her eyes wide with fear.

"Look for the girl!" a man's voice said. "Watch where you are shooting, men. Don't hit her."

It was the voice of Luke Calhoun. Caroline closed her eyes and bit her lip, not daring to believe he had come for her. She heard more shooting and more shouts, then the sound of horses galloping away from the compound.

"Colonel Calhoun, they're getting away!" someone shouted.

"Go after them. Chase the bastards back to Mexico," Luke shouted. "I'm going to look for the girl."

Caroline heard footsteps approaching the house. She sat quietly, not breathing, looking at the door.

"Miss Lafont, are you in there?" Luke called out. Caroline tried to answer but her throat was constricted, and no words came out.

"Are you all right?" Luke called again. This time, there was more anxiety in his voice.

Caroline still couldn't answer.

Suddenly, the door exploded into the room, flying off its hinges in splinters. Luke stood just on the other side of the threshold, looking in warily. Then he saw her.

"Caroline! Thank God you are all right, girl. When I didn't get an answer, I..." Luke stopped in midsentence as if he had just noticed that Caroline was wearing only her underclothing. He stood there and stared at her.

"Captain Lopez took my dress," Caroline explained. Her voice was quiet and weak.

"I'll kill the son of a bitch," Luke said. "When I catch him, I'll murder him. Any man who would force himself on a woman doesn't deserve to live."

"No, please," Caroline said. "You mustn't kill him. He didn't force himself on me."

"You say he didn't force himself on you?" Luke asked weakly.

"No," Caroline answered. "He took my dress to keep me from escaping, that's all. Would you be so kind as to find my clothes?"

"Yes, wait here, I'll find them."

"Thank you," Caroline said.

Luke went outside for a few moments and returned carrying her clothes, including the vest with the gold coins sewn inside. Had Lopez's men known about that, they would have taken the money. She was relieved to find that her gold was still safe.

"I know I no longer have any secrets from you,"

she said, "but would you allow me to dress in privacy."

"Of course," Luke said, embarrassed that she would have to request it.

———

THREE CAMPFIRES WERE STILL BURNING in the encampment when Caroline went outside and the coals still glowed in the fire where Carmelita had cooked. Caroline looked around, but she didn't see Carmelita anywhere. Then she heard hoof beats as Luke's men returned to camp, having been unsuccessful in their pursuit of Lopez.

"They got away, Colonel," one of the men said as Luke approached her.

"Why do they call you Colonel?" Caroline asked.

"Because I am a colonel in the Texas Militia," Luke said.

Caroline's voice was heavy with sarcasm. "You hold a commission in the Texas Militia. Captain Lopez holds a commission in the Mexican Army. No wonder this is a war without honor, when the likes of you and Lopez can be made officers. I thought only gentlemen could hold commissions."

"You thought wrong," Luke said, turning to one of his men. "Lieutenant McAfee, take Miss Lafont back to our settlement. Miss Lafont, you must return to New Orleans as quickly as possible."

"I told you, *Colonel*," Caroline said, leaning heavily on his military title, drawing the word out sarcastically. "I intend to press ahead until I have found my father and you can do nothing to stop me. I know where to find him now."

"I don't care how much you know, you are not going any farther," Luke said.

"You can force me to go back to your settlement if you choose to. There is nothing I can do to stop you," Caroline said. "But you had better make me your prisoner because I *intend to find my father.* I believe he is with Jim Bowie in—"

"Just a minute," Luke said, interrupting her. "What makes you think your father is with Jim Bowie?"

"Captain Lopez said Jim Bowie is fighting with the Texans. Bowie and my father are close friends. If Jim Bowie is fighting for Texas, then my father is too. Probably at his friend's side."

Luke stroked his chin and looked at her for a long moment. "Do you know Jim Bowie well enough to recognize him when you see him?" he asked.

"Of course, I do," Caroline replied. "He has been a guest in our home many times. Why are you asking me questions about Jim Bowie?"

"I have been instructed to deliver a very important message to Jim Bowie," Luke said. "If the message falls into the wrong hands, it could be disastrous."

"Colonel, I beg of you, if you are going to see Jim Bowie, please take me with you."

"You can stay with me until we find Jim Bowie," Luke said. "After that, you will return to Louisiana."

"That's wonderful," Caroline said, smiling happily. "I know my father is with Jim Bowie. And I'll be happy to go back with him."

"I expect to reach Bowie within a week," Luke said.

"Are you telling me we will find my father that soon?" Caroline asked excitedly.

"If your father is with Jim Bowie, as you believe he is, then you will see him in a week."

"Thank you," Caroline said.

"I ask only two things of you in return for taking you with me," Luke said. "First, you are to obey my commands while we are on the trail, just as if you were one of my soldiers."

"What commands?"

"All of them," Luke said. "I will not negotiate with you."

"Very well," Caroline agreed. "And the second condition?"

Luke cleared his throat. "I shall need you to point out Jim Bowie to me. As I told you, it is very important that my message be delivered to him personally but I don't know what he looks like."

"Very well, Colonel," Caroline said. "You have yourself a bargain."

"Remember," Luke said. "As soon as we find him, you will return to Louisiana."

"As soon as we find him," Caroline agreed. She was certain that Bowie and her father were together and that finding one would mean finding the other.

———

THE NEXT MORNING, bars of bright sunlight spilled in through the window and the smashed door of the cabin. A bird called impatiently outside and, in the distance, could be heard the hammering of a woodpecker. The morning sounds aroused Caroline and she found herself slowly abandoning sleep.

She was still fully dressed, having lain on the bed the night before to get what rest she could.

Caroline got out of bed and walked across the small room. The door lay in splinters where Luke had kicked it in the night before. She looked outside, blinking a few times in the brightness of the morning sun.

"Good morning," Luke said. He was squatting beside a campfire. A brace of forked twigs bracketed the fire and a green willow crosspiece straddled them. A coffee pot was suspended over the flames and Caroline could smell the aroma of the coffee as it brewed.

"Good morning," Caroline said hesitantly.

"I let you sleep late this morning," Luke explained, "because you went through quite an ordeal yesterday, being captured by the Mexicans as you were."

"Yes," Caroline replied uneasily.

"From now on, we'll have to be up and on our way before dawn," Luke went on. "That is, if you are serious about going with me."

"I'll be ready," Caroline said.

"Good. Do you want some coffee? It'll have to serve as our breakfast I'm afraid. We're traveling on short rations."

"Coffee's fine, thank you," Caroline said, accepting the empty cup Luke offered, then holding it out as he poured the rich brown liquid into it. She looked around at the white-gray residue of last night's campfires. There was not a spark left alive in any fire except the one Luke was using. "Where are the others?" she asked.

"What others?"

"Your soldiers," Caroline said, "the men who were with you."

"They've all gone back to our settlement," Luke said.

"But why? You have to deliver a message to Jim Bowie, don't you?"

"Yes, but I don't need my men to do that. They weren't a real army, anyway, just volunteers I called together to rescue you. Now that you are safe, they are free to go back to the settlement."

"How did you know I needed rescuing?"

"I figured that damn fool, Gonzara, would get you into trouble," Luke said. "So, after the two of you left, I rounded up a group of volunteers and came after you. Sure enough, we found Gonzara dead yesterday."

"Gonzara was a gentleman," Caroline defended. "I was never in any danger from him."

"Maybe not from him but you were in danger when you were with him. He did get himself killed, didn't he?"

"Yes," Caroline agreed.

"See what I mean?"

"I'm afraid I don't."

"Well, it doesn't matter. The point is, Gonzara is dead, and you are still alive, and I intend to see that you stay that way. At least until I can get you back to Louisiana."

"Just help me find my father," Caroline said. "That's all I need from you."

"Jim Bowie," Luke said. "We are looking for Jim Bowie, remember?"

"Yes," Caroline said. "I remember."

"I'm not one who approves of women dressing like men," Luke said. "But you are going to be riding a horse. It might be better if you were dressed the way you were when I first saw you."

"All right."

"I sent the horse you had pulling the carriage back with the others. I bought your horse back," Luke said. "He's tied over there with mine."

"Diablo?" Caroline said. She looked toward the tether post and saw two horses grazing quietly. One was the shiny, blue-black stallion she had brought from home. She let out a squeal of delight and ran over to the horse. Diablo nuzzled her hand. "Oh, Diablo, I'm so glad to see you."

"How glad can you be?" Luke asked sarcastically, coming up behind her "You sold him."

"I had to sell him," Caroline defended hotly. "I needed the carriage to search for my father."

"Tell that to your horse," Luke said. "I'm not the one you have to explain yourself to."

"You're right," Caroline said. "I don't have to explain anything to you."

Caroline turned away from him and went inside the cabin to change her clothes.

A few minutes later, Caroline went back outside, dressed in men's clothes. Luke had already saddled his own horse and was just finishing with hers. He tied her bag to the saddle horn.

"Let's go," he said, swinging up into his own saddle and starting off at a canter without looking back.

Caroline quickly mounted the blue-black stallion and caught up with Luke Calhoun as he reined Traveler into a walk. "You misrepresented yourself back in the settlement," she said accusingly. "You didn't say anything about being in the army."

"I didn't say I wasn't," Luke said.

"You told me this was a war with no right, only wrong," Caroline said.

"That's right."

"Then how can you be a part of it?"

"Because the Texans aren't as wrong as the Mexicans," Luke said.

"I don't understand what this war is about."

"It's simple enough," Luke said. "Americans have come here and turned desert country into farms and ranches. The Mexicans weren't interested in working the land. They just wanted to hold on to it. Then, when they saw the Americans making something out of it, they wanted their share."

"If it was their land to begin with, they have a right to hold on to it, don't they?" Caroline asked.

"It's not the Mexicans' land anymore," Luke said. "Most of the land the Americans are living on is acreage they bought fair and square. The Mexicans aren't disputing that but they are making it hard for the Americans to live here. They're charging taxes and they're passing laws against us. We're left with no voice in the government that controls us. A little like the colonies were before Independence. The truth is, there probably aren't half a dozen Texans who were born here but, once they got here, they staked out a claim and that was that. Now, those Texans are fighting their own war for independence. Texas is going to be a nation. The bad part of that is, there are a lot of Mexicans living here who don't want independence. That's the wrong of it from the Texans' side."

"Why are people like Jim Bowie and my father mixed up in it?" Caroline asked. "It isn't their war."

"Bowie probably has a thousand or so acres at stake here in Texas. If we win this war, he'll be a rich man. Your father, too, I reckon."

"My father already owns land in Louisiana," Caroline said.

"Didn't you say you are here right now to keep someone from stealing that land?"

"My father's partner."

"Maybe your father came here to find a piece of land that no one could take away from him. Who knows what drives men to fight in this war?"

"What about you?" Caroline asked. "Why are you here?"

"I don't know," Luke admitted. "I guess I just wanted to see the elephant."

They rode in silence, after that, for the better part of the morning. Caroline looked out over the wide-open spaces before her. Surely there was enough land here for anyone who wanted it. It seemed to her there was enough land to give to every man, woman, and child in the United States, and still have land left over. How could this war be justified? The land in Texas was limitless.

They stopped to rest at midday. Luke killed a rabbit and they cooked it over an open fire. To Caroline's surprise, it tasted quite good. They rode all afternoon, stopping when they reached a river, where Luke caught two fish for their supper.

"Where do you live?" Caroline asked as they ate their supper.

"Here," Luke answered, making a sweep with his hands.

"You mean out in the wild?"

"Yes," Luke said.

"Don't you ever miss having a home? Wouldn't you like to have a family?"

"A man like me has no business thinking about a home and family."

"You mean you never intend to get married?"

"No."

Luke's answer was short and direct and left no room for further discussion.

"We'd better bed down," Luke said. "We've got a long ride ahead of us tomorrow and you won't be able to sleep late as you did this morning. We'll have to get under way before dawn. We can spread our blankets out in the grass over there."

She lay down and looked up at the brilliant stars that sparkled above. Luke had been right about the grass. It made a soft bed, softer even than the real bed she had slept in the night before.

"Ouch!" Luke said. "Damn!"

"What's wrong?"

"I spread my blanket on some prickly pear cactus."

Caroline laughed. "Even I know better than to sleep in a bed of cactus, Colonel Calhoun."

Luke pulled his blanket some distance away and spread it out again. A few minutes after he had stretched out on it, he began complaining about the rocks beneath his shoulders. Caroline chuckled. "Good night, Colonel Calhoun."

"Good night, Miss Lafont."

Caroline lay quietly for several moments, looking at the stars spread out in the vast, cathedral vault above.

"There is this to be said about your mode of living, Colonel," she finally said. "No bedroom could ever have a lovelier ceiling. The stars are absolutely beautiful."

"Yes," Luke said, "they are."

Chapter 7

They were up before dawn the next day and had been on the trail for an hour before the sun peeked up over the edge of the distant horizon, sending bars of light out to push away the darkness.

Luke was a hard rider but he rested his horse often and saw to it that both mounts got sufficient water. When the sun reached its apex, they both dismounted and walked beside the stallions.

It was after dark when they quit the trail and wiped down the horses. Caroline slept the sleep of the exhausted that night.

After dark on the fifth day, Caroline was rubbing her bottom gingerly when Luke told her he had a surprise.

"We're going to have beans for supper," he said. "I thought a slight change in fare would be good for us."

"Impossible," Caroline said. "You have to soak beans for a long time before you cook them. Otherwise they're no good."

"I've been soaking them ever since last night,"

Luke said, smiling. He took a pouch from the pommel of his saddle. "I put some beans in this skin last night and covered them with water. We can have them cooked in less than an hour. I found some peppers, too."

"Oh, Luke, that sounds wonderful," Caroline said. "Not that I haven't been grateful for the game you've provided, mind you. It's just that I was beginning to wonder if I would ever eat anything besides wild meat again."

Luke laughed. "I get to feeling that way myself sometimes," he said. "I always buy beans when I can. Or corn, or peas. It's good to have a little variety."

"I'll gather some firewood," Caroline offered.

"Good. I'll take care of the horses."

Caroline went about gathering firewood while, behind her, Luke tended to the horses.

There were things about this life that Caroline did like. She loved the sounds at night. The birds and insects and frogs seemed to sing their nightly music just for her. And she loved looking at the brilliant points of light far overhead. The stars were so distant and so cold-looking. She wondered what made them glow. Sometimes a star fell to earth. Her father's friend, Jim Bowie, had made his famous knife, the knife they named after him, from the metal found in a fallen star. Caroline had seen that star and it looked just like a piece of rock to her. It didn't glow at all. Why did stars glow when they were fixed in the sky? And what held them up there?

Caroline returned to the campsite with an armload of wood and she dropped it inside the circle of rocks Luke had fashioned. He used his flint and tinder and, in a few minutes, he had a fire going. He suspended a pot above the flames and began to cook the beans.

In the distance, a coyote howled. Luke saw Caroline shiver and moved over to sit beside her.

"It's just a coyote," he said.

"They sound so mournful."

"That's just the way we think they sound. The truth is, that's a happy yell. That coyote has his mate with him and he's telling everyone about it. Like this."

Luke cupped his hand to one side of his mouth and let out a yelping howl, much like the coyote's, complete with the long, mournful wail at the end.

Despite herself, Caroline laughed.

They ate a leisurely meal and Caroline could not remember when she had tasted anything more delicious.

———

THE NEXT MORNING, when Caroline returned to the camp after her morning toilet, she found Luke already up and dressed and both horses saddled.

"I overslept," he said. "You should have awakened me."

"I'm sorry," Caroline said. "I wanted the chance to bathe in the stream."

"Yes, well, you've done that. Now, we must go. We are to meet Bowie today."

"Today?" Caroline said.

"Yes, the information I have is that he will be in a saloon on the other side of the Brazos—today."

She wondered if her father would be there with

Bowie. If he was not, what then? Would Luke send her back to Louisiana?

"I'll water the horses," Luke said. He walked the two stallions down to the stream, while Caroline, confused by the mixed emotions she was experiencing, got dressed.

They crossed the Brazos in midafternoon. The river lay before them, bright and shining, flowing majestically. At this point, it was shallow enough to promise an easy crossing.

A small log building stood on the other side of the river. Even from where she stood, Caroline could see the crudely lettered sign that identified the cabin as the Brazos Crossing Saloon. She could also see half a dozen horses tied up out front.

"Well, someone is there," Luke said as they reached the bank of the river and stood gazing across at the saloon. "If we are lucky, it will be our man."

Luke rode slowly out into the water but Caroline did not move. After a moment, Luke realized she wasn't behind him and he turned his horse and rode back to her. "What's wrong?" he asked, gently.

Caroline started to speak and was surprised to feel a hard lump in her throat. Tears flooded her eyes, then began to track down over her cheeks.

"Caroline?" Luke said in surprise. "What is it? Why are you crying?"

"Luke, what will happen in that saloon?"

"If Bowie is there, I'll give him my message and my mission will be finished. If your father is there, then your search will be over. After that, I suppose we'll go our separate ways."

"What if Bowie is there and my father isn't?"

"Caroline, you must prepare yourself for that possibility," Luke said. "We can only hope your father will be with Bowie."

"If he isn't...Luke, will you help me find him?"

"Caroline, that depends on what Jim Bowie has to say," Luke said. "If he has orders for me, I must follow them. If he has no orders, then I will be free to do as I choose."

"And you will help me find my father?"

"I'm crazy for saying this, but, yes, I'll help you," Luke said.

Caroline smiled. "Thank you."

"Now, will you ride across the river with me?"

"Yes," Caroline said.

"And dry your eyes," he said gently. "Whether Bowie and your father are there or not, I don't want to be seen riding in with a partner who is crying. Remember you're passing yourself off as a man."

"Wait!" Luke said, holding up his arm quickly, to stop them.

"What is it?" Caroline asked.

"Look at the saddles of those horses," Luke said. "See the silver conchas? Those are Mexican saddles."

"That doesn't necessarily mean anything, does it?" Caroline asked.

"No," Luke admitted. "There are lots of Mexicans around who don't want anything to do with the war. And there are even more Mexican saddles. Still, it seems a little odd to see so many of them together in the same place."

"Do you think there's something wrong?"

"I don't know. Caroline, you stay out here and let

me go in first. If everything is all right, I'll come out and get you."

"No," Caroline answered. "What if something goes wrong?"

"If that happens, I'll have a better chance of defending myself if I don't have you to worry about."

"But I—" Caroline started.

"Don't argue," Luke said. "Just stay out here. If you hear any shooting, you get the hell out of here. The message I have for Bowie is from Sam Houston. I'm going to tell you what it is. If something does happen to me, I want you to get it to Bowie. Will you do that for me?"

"Yes," Caroline said softly. "But Luke, *please* be careful."

"I will be," Luke promised. "Now, here's the message: Tell Bowie that Houston does not want the Texans to defend the Alamo. Have you got that? Houston believes that the only way to defend Texas is to operate as a mobile army, hitting the enemy hard, then falling back and hitting them again, just as we defeated the British sixty years ago. We don't have the strength to hold a defensive position."

"What is the Alamo?" Caroline asked.

"It's an old church in Bexar that Colonel Neill and some others have turned into a fort," Luke said. "Just exactly what we don't want. Niel has to be persuaded to abandon it and Bowie has to take the orders to him."

"All right," Caroline agreed. "I'll tell him."

"Stay on this side of the river until you see me wave. If anything goes wrong, the river will slow them down enough to give you a good start."

"Be careful," Caroline said again.

Caroline patted Diablo's neck while Luke forded the shallow river. She watched him dismount and walk into the saloon. She held her breath for a long moment, then let out a sigh of relief when he reappeared and waved her over.

She squeezed her heels against Diablo's side and the stallion cantered into the water sending sheets of silver spray flying to either side.

Caroline tethered Diablo in front of the saloon and went inside. The inside of the building was so dark that it was difficult to see at first and she had to let her eyes adjust to the dim light. Finally, she saw Luke sitting at a table near the back of the room and she went over to sit with him. Almost immediately, the saloon owner put glasses of whiskey in front of them.

"I can't drink whiskey," Caroline protested.

"Just pretend to drink it," Luke said. "I'll switch glasses with you in a moment."

"All right," Caroline said. She held the glass up to her lips. Even though she didn't open her mouth, she could feel the fire of the pungent liquid on her lips.

"Is Mr. Bowie here?" she asked.

"He's out back," Luke said.

"My father?"

"I'll let you ask him that."

They sat at the table for a few minutes longer and Luke, as he promised, switched glasses with Caroline. Finally, the back door opened and a man came in.

"Who in here is looking for Jim Bowie?" the man called out.

"Those two men at that table," the saloonkeeper said, pointing to Luke and Caroline.

"I'm Jim Bowie," the man said, smiling broadly and showing a gold tooth. "What do you want?"

Beneath the table, Caroline put her hand on Luke's leg and squeezed it tightly.

"What is it?" Luke asked under his breath.

"That isn't Jim Bowie," she said.

Caroline felt Luke's leg muscles tense under her hand. Then she saw his arm move and realized he had drawn his pistol. He was pointing the pistol at the man's stomach, though the table masked his move.

"My friend tells me you aren't Jim Bowie," Luke said.

"Your friend is a liar," the man said, menacingly.

"I tend to believe my friend unless you can prove otherwise," Luke said. "If you are Jim Bowie, let me see some proof. Show me your knife."

"I'll show you my knife, you Texas bastard," the man spat. "Kill 'em both, boys. They *know!*"

The man reached for his gun but Luke's pistol roared before he could draw. A hole appeared in the man's chest as the ball from Luke's gun smashed into him. His shirt flooded red and he coughed as he fell.

Two men at the bar turned toward Caroline and Luke and fired their pistols. One of the balls came so close to Caroline that she felt it as it whizzed past. The other one tore into Luke's shoulder and she heard him grunt in pain as the force of the blow slammed him against the wall.

The men's pistols had to be muzzle loaded and neither Luke nor the two ruffians at the bar had time to reload for a second shot.

"You take the little one," one of the men shouted,

pulling his knife as he started toward Luke and Caroline. "I'll gut the big son of a bitch!"

Caroline looked at them in horror as they started toward her. Both were holding wicked-looking knives and she knew that, in a second, she and Luke would be ripped to pieces.

"Caroline, the pistol," Luke gasped, pointing to the weapon dropped by the counterfeit Jim Bowie.

Caroline seized the pistol and handed it to Luke. He aimed it at the nearest attacker and shot him as he lunged for Caroline. A hole appeared in the man's forehead as he tumbled over backwards.

A second shot rang out at almost the same moment and the face of the second man, who had raised his knife against Luke, suddenly assumed an expression of surprise. Then, slowly, he tumbled forward, dropping his knife with a clatter. A gaping wound yawned in the back of his head.

Caroline looked toward the bar in surprise and saw the saloonkeeper holding the smoking rifle that had saved Luke's life.

"I'm sorry I told you this here fella was Jim Bowie," the saloon owner said to Luke. "He told me that's who he was and, as I never met Jim Bowie, I had no reason not to believe him."

Luke stood up painfully, using his good hand to try to stanch the flow of blood from his shoulder wound. Despite his efforts, the blood poured through his fingers.

"I accept your apology," Luke said. "And I offer you my thanks." He looked down at the three dead men. "They were all Texans," he said. "Why did they attack us?"

"No, by God, they warn't Texans," the saloon-keeper said, spitting contemptuously on one of the bodies. "They was spyin' for the Mexicans but I don't reckon any self- respectin' Mex would want to claim 'em, any more'n we would. They was scum, sellin' their souls to the highest bidder. Like as not, that one was posin' as Jim Bowie so's to be able to get some information from you."

"If it hadn't been for my friend here," Luke said, nodding toward Caroline, "they would have been successful. Fortunately, my friend knows Jim Bowie and recognized this impostor for what he was."

"Yeah, well, I guess you got that to thank him for," the man said, looking at Caroline critically. "He ain't worth much in a fight, though, is he?"

"It was his first fight," Luke said. "He'll be all right the next time."

"There damn near warn't no next time," the saloon owner said.

Luke picked up his hat and put it on, then holstered his pistol and shoved the dead impostor's gun inside his belt.

"You got anything I can use to make a bandage?" he asked.

"The missus has some quiltin' material," the barman said. "I'll fetch it."

Luke walked over to the bar and took down a bottle of whiskey. "I reckon I'll have to be obliged to you to dig this ball out of my shoulder." He pulled the cork out of the whiskey bottle with his teeth and took a long drink of the fiery liquid.

"I reckon I can do that," the saloonkeeper said. "It won't be the first ball I've pulled out."

"Hurry, will you?" Luke asked. "I've got to find Bowie."

Luke raised the bottle for a second drink but he never made it. Caroline saw his eyelids flutter. Then he dropped the bottle and with a groan, collapsed.

"Luke!" Caroline screamed.

"That's a pretty strong fella," the barman said laconically. "I was wonderin' when he was gonna pass out. Most of 'em would've gone under long before this."

"Will he be all right?" Caroline asked.

"He'll live," the barkeeper said. "I'll get the missus. She'll take care of him."

Chapter 8

Luke opened his eyes and tried to sit up but the abrupt movement sent a searing stab of pain through his shoulder. He gasped and fell back on the bed.

"Be still," Caroline said. "If you move so abruptly you will open the wound again."

Luke looked around the room, then let his eyes settle on Caroline's face. She could see that they were clouded with confusion as well as with pain.

"Where are we?" Luke asked.

"In the saloonkeeper's house," Caroline said.

Luke tried to sit up again. "We can't stay here, Caroline. We've got to get the Texans out of the Alamo, don't you understand? If they hole up there, they'll be killed to the man!"

"You can't go anywhere," Caroline said. "You are too badly wounded. If you try to travel, you'll die."

By sheer effort of will, Luke managed to swing his feet over the side of the bed but, when he tried to stand, he was overtaken by dizziness and nausea and he passed out again.

Caroline managed to get him back in bed, then she moved her chair to sit beside him.

The saloonkeeper's wife—a heavy-set woman named Nellie—heard the commotion and hurried into the bedroom to see what was going on.

"Your friend tried to get up, did he?"

"Yes," Caroline answered, looking anxiously into Luke's face. "He's determined to travel to a fort called the Alamo. Have you ever heard of it?"

"The Alamo, yes, I know where it is," the woman said. "It's at San Antonio de Béxar, near the San Antonio River."

"How far is it from here?"

"It's a good distance—maybe a week of hard riding," Nellie said. "I went once by wagon. That was near a month."

"I'm going there," Caroline said. "I've got to warn them for him."

"It'd be a rough trip for a woman," Nellie said.

"What?" Caroline gasped.

Nellie chuckled. "Did you think I didn't know?"

"Who else knows?"

"If you're lucky, no one else knows," Nellie said. "I reckon no one else has seen you look into your man's face the way I have. You love him, don't you?"

"Yes," Caroline admitted.

"I figure a love like that has got to be returned so he probably loves you just as much as you love him. That means he ain't gonna let you go."

"He's not going to find out," Caroline said. "I'll leave while he's asleep."

"That won't make no difference," Nellie said. "He'll know you went on and he'll try to go after you. And like as not, it'll kill him."

"He won't follow me if he thinks I've returned to Louisiana," Caroline said. She took a deep breath. "When he awakens, tell him I grew frightened and went back home. Tell him I said I couldn't take this sort of life anymore."

"If I tell him that, he won't give you credit for much gumption," Nellie warned.

"I know," Caroline said.

"Is that what you want?"

"I want him to stay here until he is well enough to travel. Maybe if he thinks I have gone back, he will be so dispirited that he won't feel like moving."

"On the other hand, he may think there's nothin' worth livin' for anymore. That could be all the reason he needs to go on to Béxar."

"I've thought of that, too," Caroline said. "Tell him Lieutenant McAfee came through here and took the message on to San Antonio."

"Lieutenant McAfee?"

"Yes," Caroline said. "Lieutenant McAfee is one of his most trusted men. Luke will be satisfied that all is being done that can be done."

"Seems to me like the smartest thing for you to do would be to go back and get this McAfee and send him on to Béxar," Nellie suggested.

"No," Caroline said. "It's a long ride back to the settlement. It would take me two weeks to go there and three weeks for McAfee to travel to the Alamo. In five weeks, it will be too late. I've got to go on to Béxar myself." Caroline reached into the secret slit of her vest, pulled out two gold coins, and handed them to Nellie. "This should be enough to see to his care," she said. Nellie looked at the money and smiled broadly. "Dearie, this is more money than we've seen all year," she said. "It is more than enough to take care of your man."

"And convince him that I have gone back to Louisiana and that Lieutenant McAfee carried his message on to the Alamo?"

"Yes," Nellie said. "It is enough for me to convince him that as well."

Luke groaned.

"He's waking up again," Nellie said. "You won't be able to leave while he is awake."

"I know," Caroline said. "I'll give him whiskey. We'll get him so drunk that he'll pass out again, this time for a long while. By the time he wakes up, I will be gone."

"I'll get the whiskey," Nellie said.

By the time Luke regained consciousness a few moments later, Caroline was waiting for him with a whiskey bottle and an empty glass.

"What happened?" Luke asked. "Did I pass out again?"

"Yes," Caroline said. She forced a laugh. "How are you going to lead a rescue mission if you can't even stand up?"

"I've got to try," Luke said. Once again, he tried to sit up.

"All right, if you insist, we'll go on to San Antonio," Caroline said. "But first, I want you to drink this. You need it to help you fight the wound."

"Whiskey?"

"Yes."

"I thought you didn't approve of whiskey."

"This is for medicinal purposes," Caroline said, handing him the glass she had filled.

"Oh, well," Luke said, managing a smile despite the pain, "if it is for medicinal purposes..." He drank the whiskey without protest.

"Have another," she said, refilling the glass.

"I don't mind if I do." Luke drank the second glassful, then wiped his mouth with the back of his hand.

"Do you think you could hold another?" Caroline asked, pouring again.

Luke smiled. "Madam, do you know whom you are talking to?" he asked. "I mean, to whom you are talking to?" he slurred, trying to get the correct phrase. He giggled and reached for the glass. He turned it up and drained it, then held it out for another refill.

"Colonel, I must say, you have an amazing capacity for John Barleycorn," Caroline said as she filled the glass a fourth time. The bottle had been nearly three-quarters full when they started. This emptied it.

"I'm feeling pretty good now," Luke slurred. "The pain's all gone. This was a good idea. We can get started right away. By night, we'll be a long way from here."

"I need a little more whiskey," he said, holding up his empty glass. "For medicinal purposes," he slurred.

Caroline looked at Nellie in confusion as if to ask what she should do next.

"I'll get some more," Nellie said.

"No, never mind, I'll get it myself," Luke said and he stood up beside the bed. At that moment, his eyelids dropped shut and he fell back on the bed, out cold.

Nellie rushed over to him and opened one eyelid. "Whew," she said. "I never saw a man could hold so much liquor, so fast. All right, dearie, he's out now, and he's likely to sleep until this time tomorrow. If you're gonna leave, now's the time to do it."

"Thank you," Caroline said. "We owe a lot to you and your husband. You have saved our lives."

"We're Texans," the woman said as if that explained everything.

Nellie gave Caroline some food to carry with her and Caroline was grateful because she knew she wouldn't be able to supplement her diet with game as had Luke.

She rode hard the first day, not only because she was in a hurry to carry the warning to the Alamo, but also because she wanted to get far enough away so that there would be no chance of Luke's coming after her. She slept under the stars the first night and was surprised at how familiar she found it. Her time with Luke had made her at ease in the wild and when she went to sleep that night to the sound of a coyote's distant cry, she felt not the slightest twinge of fear. Three days of traveling brought her to another saloon, not unlike the one in which she had left Luke. She had no wish to drink but a saloon meant people, and people meant information.

She went inside and sat down at a rough-hewn table near the back wall. When the barkeeper came to see to her order she asked, "Do you serve meals?"

The saloon owner chuckled. "That's a pretty way of askin'," he said. "You from the East or somethin'?"

Caroline knew she had to watch her language and expressions. She shouldn't call attention to herself in any way and the refined phraseology she used did just that. "Yeah," she said in a low grunt.

"Well, we ain't got no meals exactly," he said, accenting the word *meals*. "But we got some beans. Would you like some beans?"

"Yeah," Caroline said.

"Whiskey?"

"Yeah," Caroline said again. How she longed for a little wine but she knew better than to ask for it.

A plate of beans and a piece of hard bread appeared in front of her a few moments later along with a glass of whiskey. Caroline looked at the food, remembering the beans she had shared with Luke on the trail a few days ago.

When she was halfway through her meal, a man entered the saloon—a tall man with the same look of strength and determination Caroline had seen in Luke. He was, however, considerably older than Luke and Caroline, had she been asked to guess his age, would have put him in his late thirties, as old as Jim Bowie, and very nearly as old as her father. He took off his hat and slapped it against his trousers, raising a cloud of trail dust. He looked around the room, then walked up to the bar.

"Howard, give me whiskey," he said.

"Ben Nichols," the saloonkeeper exclaimed, as he poured a glass of whiskey. "What brings you here?"

"I'm recruitin' for Colonel Neill," Ben Nichols said.

"The last time I seen you, you was with Henri Lafont," the barman said, conversationally.

Caroline stood up so quickly that her chair fell over

backwards with a crash. Ben Nichols whirled to face her, one hand on his pistol. The saloon owner ducked behind the bar and the four or five others in the room all dived to the floor.

Fortunately for Caroline, Ben saw that she wasn't armed, so he didn't shoot. But he didn't take his hand off the pistol, either.

"Mister, you better have a good reason why you jolted me like that," Ben said coldly.

"Did he—did he say you were with Henri Lafont?"

"Yeah, he said that," Ben said. "You got a quarrel with Henri? 'Cause if you do, I'm afraid you're gonna have to come through me first. Henri is my friend."

"Then he is alive?"

"Of course he's still alive," Ben said. "Leastwise he was last week when I left him. What do you want with him?"

"He is my father," Caroline said.

"You're lyin' through your teeth, mister," Ben said menacingly. "Henri has three daughters, no sons. And if he did have a boy, I doubt he would have one as delicate as you."

Caroline took off her hat and let her hair fall loose. She shook her head until her hair cascaded down over her shoulders. "I am his oldest daughter."

"Well, I'll be damned, would you look at that?" said one of the men who had dived to the floor to avoid what they thought was going to be a gunfight. He got up slowly, as did the others. There was a general shuffle of tables and chairs as the men sat down to watch the drama developing before them.

Ben Nichols removed his hand from his holster.

"Would you be the one he calls Caroline?" he asked.

"Yes," Caroline answered happily. "Oh, you do know my father."

"Girl, what are you doing here?" Ben Nichols asked. "Henri thinks you and your sisters and your mother are safe, back in Louisiana."

"It's a long story," Caroline said. "Mr. Nichols, I must find my father. We are in danger of losing everything we have if we can't prove he is alive."

"Prove he is alive? Why, he's written to you just about every week," Ben said. "I've carried some of his letters myself."

"But, that's impossible," Caroline said. "We've never heard a word."

"He has sent them in care of Frank Sweeny, his business partner," Ben said.

"Oh," Caroline said, "I should have known what a snake Mr. Sweeny was. He has hidden the letters so he can prove his claim."

"What claim is that?"

"If we can't prove my father is alive, Mr. Sweeny will get control of all our property. There is an old agreement he and my father entered into before my parents were ever married."

"Surely your father made a different agreement later on?"

"If so, no one can find it," Caroline said.

"If this Frank Sweeny is hidin' your father's letters, then it wouldn't be beyond him to hide the new agreement, too," Ben said. "So, you want to go to your father, do you?"

"Yes," Caroline said. "Oh, no, I can't! At least, not yet."

"Why not?"

"There is something I must do," Caroline said.

"Something more important than findin' your own father?"

"I wouldn't have thought so last week," Caroline said. "In fact, I wouldn't even have thought so a few days ago. But now, I must go to a place called the Alamo."

"Why?" Ben asked, suspiciously.

"I have to carry a message to my father's old friend, Jim Bowie," Caroline said.

"What's the message?"

"It's ..." Caroline started to tell him, then stopped. Maybe she shouldn't. Luke had said the message was for Jim Bowie only. And yet, Luke had trusted her because he had to. Was it any different for her to trust this Ben Nichols? Besides, he was a friend of her father's, so it couldn't possibly be wrong to tell him.

"Go on, girl," Ben said. "What message do you have for Jim Bowie?"

"General Houston wants Colonel Neill to abandon the Alamo," Caroline said. "He says all Texas soldiers should be united into one mobile army and none should be left behind in static defenses. He is afraid that any attempt to defend the Alamo will result in total annihilation for the defenders."

"The Alamo is almost a week's journey from here," Ben said. "And General Santa Anna's army has it totally surrounded. If you try and get there, the chances are very good that you'll be captured."

"I've got to take that chance," Caroline said.

Ben looked at her stoically, then he drank his whiskey. He wiped the back of his hand across his mouth and smiled.

"I'll take you there," he said.

"Oh, thank you," Caroline said. "You are very kind. And then, if it isn't too much to ask, would you take me to my father as well? I'll gladly pay you for your time and trouble."

"Miss Caroline, you don't understand," Ben said, smiling at her. "When I take you to the Alamo, I will be taking you to your father. He's one of the defenders."

"My father is fighting with the Texans? But why?"

"Because he is a true patriot," Ben said.

Caroline shook her head. "Mr. Nichols, there are many things about my father that I don't understand."

———

IT WASN'T JUST the whiskey that kept Luke in bed for the next three days. Infection set in around his wound and he developed a high fever. He lay in bed, semiconscious, and fought the illness that racked his body.

In his delirium, he suffered hallucinations so real that he could not discern the difference between the dream and reality.

Ad sat on the bed and bathed his head with a cool cloth. She was very pretty, a sweet, innocent girl of seventeen. She was wearing the dress she had worn on the day she and Luke were married, the same dress, in fact, that she had been buried in.

"Adriana," Luke said. He tried to sit up but Adriana pushed him back down.

"No," she said, sweetly. "You mustn't try to get up now. You must rest."

"What are you doing here?" Luke asked. "I don't understand."

"Did you say something, Colonel Calhoun?" Nellie asked, coming into the bedroom. Her apron and her hands were covered with flour.

Luke looked at Nellie, then at the bed where he had seen Adriana. There was no one there.

"I thought—" Luke said. He stopped. If he told her he thought he had seen his wife, she would think he was crazy. And perhaps he was because Adriana had been dead for three years, killed by two men who had found her alone in the cabin. She had fought them with a butcher knife, displaying the fury of a lioness protecting her cubs. She was still alive when Luke returned home and she told him how she had marked them. One man had lost an ear to her attack. She had branded the other with a cross, slashed on his cheek. She died in Luke's arms as he swore to her that he would find the two men and kill them.

Nellie held her hand to Luke's face. He could smell the flour she was working with and, for a moment, it reminded him of his mother when he was very young.

"Hmm," Nellie said. "Your fever seems to have broken, Colonel Calhoun. I think the worst is over."

Even as she spoke, Luke was aware that the pounding dizziness had passed. He looked around the room.

"How long have I been like this?" he asked.

"About four days," Nellie answered.

"Caroline?" Luke asked. "Where is she?"

Nellie laughed. "That one sure didn't have much grit. She hightailed it home to Louisiana."

"What?"

"Yes, sir she said she'd seen enough of shootin' and the like. She give me some money to nurse you and home she went."

Luke felt a pang of disappointment, not only because Caroline was gone but also because she had not exhibited the character he thought she possessed. He sighed sadly.

"Would you hand me my boots, please? I have to press on."

"You mean to Bexar?"

Luke looked up in surprise.

"Oh, I know all about the message you were supposed to deliver to Colonel Bowie," she said. "Lieutenant McAfee came by here before Miss Caroline left. He took the message on to Bexar himself."

"McAfee was by here? I don't remember that."

"I guess not," Nellie said. "You were unconscious."

"You're sure he took the message?"

Nellie patted his hand comfortingly. "Don't you worry, Colonel, your message is in good hands. You just get yourself well again."

Luke wondered what he should do now. Without the message to deliver, he had no mission. And without Caroline, he realized, he had no future.

Chapter 9

As Luke rode away from the saloon, back toward the settlement, he tried to force his thoughts away from Caroline. If he thought of her too much, he would drive himself crazy. She had gone back to Louisiana. Whatever he thought he had seen in her obviously wasn't there because she hadn't even stayed with him long enough to see if he would survive the wound he had suffered.

No matter how hard he tried to forget about Caroline, she kept creeping back into his thoughts. He would hear a splashing brook and think of her laugh or the song of wind in the trees would remind him of her gentle sighs. Once a bird called and he turned in his saddle, believing she had spoken his name.

———

To get his mind off Caroline, he began to think of his late wife, Adriana, and their bittersweet marriage. As a wedding gift, Don Pedro Romero, Adriana's father, had doubled the number of acres Luke had purchased from him, putting Luke in position to be one of the wealthiest American ranchers in Texas.

Then, one day he went with Don Pedro to the Mexican state of Sonora to examine a new breed of cattle reputed to thrive in the Texas climate. When he returned to his own home, he found Adriana dying. She had been attacked the day before, she said, by two Americans. She had fought them but they finally managed to subdue her. Then they had beaten her and left her to die. She lived less than two hours after Luke found her.

In his grief, Luke had given all his land back to Don Pedro. He burned the house he had built for Adriana, then he went after the two men who had murdered her.

Less than a week after he buried Adriana, Luke stopped at a saloon in a small Texas town. The saloon owner stood at the end of the bar. There were two glasses with whiskey remaining in them and he poured the whiskey back into a bottle, corked it, and put it on a shelf behind the bar. He wiped the glasses out with his stained apron, then set them among the unused glasses. He saw Luke step up to the bar and he moved down toward him.

"Whiskey," Luke said.

The barman reached for the bottle he had just poured the whiskey back into but Luke pointed to an unopened bottle.

"That one," he said.

The saloonkeeper shrugged and pulled the cork from the fresh bottle.

"I'm looking for two men," Luke said.

"Mister, mostly what I do is mind my own business."

"They'll be scarred," Luke said. "One bears a cross on his face and the other has just lost an ear."

The barkeeper didn't say anything but Luke noticed a slight reaction to his description.

"Last week they murdered my wife," Luke said.

The bartender looked up. "Would your wife's name have been Adriana?" he asked.

Hearing his wife's name spoken by this stranger made Luke's head light and he had to take a quick breath to steady himself.

"How do you know?" he said.

"A couple of hombres traded this for whiskey and two women," the saloonkeeper said. He picked up a gold locket and Luke recognized it as the one Romero had given his daughter on their wedding day. Adriana's name was engraved on the back.

"One of them said the locket belonged to his mother," the barman said. "When I asked him what his mother's name was, he said Sarah. He couldn't read, you see, and he had no idea what was inscribed here."

"It's hers," Luke said in a choked voice. "Where are they?"

The saloon owner said nothing but he raised his head and looked toward the stairs at the back of the room.

"Thanks," Luke said.

At the back of the saloon, a flight of wooden stairs led up to an enclosed loft. Luke guessed that the two doors at the head of the stairs led to the rooms used by the prostitutes who worked in the saloon.

Luke pulled his knife from his belt sheath and started toward the stairs.

The dozen or more men in the saloon had been talking and laughing among themselves. When they saw Luke pull his knife, their conversation died, and they watched him walk quietly up the steps.

From the rooms above him, he could hear muffled sounds that left little doubt as to what was going on behind the closed doors. Normally, such sounds called forth ribald comments from the patrons below but now there was no teasing whatever. Everyone knew that a life-and-death confrontation was about to take place. No one knew why but then, such things occurred often and no one really cared about the reasons.

Luke tried to open the first door but it was locked. He knocked on it.

"Go 'way, Joiner," a man's voice called from the other side of the door. "You've had your woman, now let me have mine."

Luke knocked again.

"Dammit, Joiner, I said go 'way!"

Luke took one step back from the door then raised his foot and kicked it hard. The door flew open with a crash and the woman inside the room screamed.

"What the hell?" the man shouted. He stood up quickly and Luke saw a bloodstained bandage over his ear.

His blood raced! This was one of them!

"Do you have a knife, mister?" Luke said coldly.

The woman tried to cover herself with the quilt. She looked at Luke with fear in her eyes.

"Get out of here before you get hurt," Luke said to the woman.

Whimpering in fear, the woman hurried past Luke. She dropped the quilt on the floor, then ran down the stairs, totally naked. Such a thing would have normally brought peals of laughter from those below but their eyes were glued on Luke, who was still standing out on the landing, and they barely noticed the naked woman.

"Who are you?" the man asked. "What do you want?"

Luke pointed to the man's ear. "I mean to finish the job my wife started on you."

"You're crazy. What are you talking about?"

"How did you lose your ear?"

"I was in a fight—" the man started to say.

Luke interrupted. "Some fight," he said. "Two of you against one woman. She described both of you to me before she died and—"

"She died?" the man asked weakly. His face grew ashen. "Mister, we didn't intend to kill her just to rough her up a little."

"Yeah?" Luke answered. "Well, I don't intend to rough you up a little, just to kill you. Now get a knife or, by God, I'll kill you where you stand."

"I don't have a knife," the man said. He came toward Luke with his hands stretched out in front of him. "Please, don't kill me, mister."

At the last instant, the pleading expression left his face to be replaced by an evil grin and Luke saw that the man did hold a knife in his hand. Somehow, he had managed to hide it from him until he was close enough to make one stomach-opening swipe. The man lunged and Luke barely managed to avoid the point of the knife. One inch closer and he would have been disemboweled.

"I'll cut you open like a pig, you son of a bitch! I'll pay you back for what your wife did to my ear!"

The man swung again and Luke jumped deftly to one side, then lunged forward. The blade of his knife buried itself in the man's neck and Luke felt his hot blood spilling across his hand.

The man gurgled and his eyes bulged open wide. Then, slowly, he slipped to the floor dead.

Luke pulled his knife from the man's neck. He heard a sound behind him and turned quickly to look into the green, hate-filled, fear-crazed eyes of the other man. A great cross-shaped wound marked the man's right cheek.

The man drew his arm and hurled his knife. Luke leaned to one side and the knife whizzed past, then sank into the wall behind him. The cross-scarred man, weaponless now, vaulted over the railing to the floor below. He landed on a table as gracefully as a cat, then jumped to the floor and escaped through the front door.

Luke ran down the stairs and out the door but the man was nowhere in sight. From that day forward, he had kept looking for him. He had heard the first man call him Joiner but he didn't know if that was a first name, last name, or nickname. It didn't matter anyway. People could change names as easily as they changed shirts. But this man could never change the flat green eyes Luke had looked into. And he would always bear the cross-shaped scar Adriana had put on his face.

Luke no longer pursued him with the same, dogged determination. He had realized that he would have to go on living. And he had learned, just days ago, that it was even possible for him to love again. The girl, Caroline, had moved him in ways he had not thought possible anymore. But then she had disappointed him by leaving Texas, by abandoning her search for her father. Although Luke had repeatedly urged her to return to Louisiana, he had secretly admired her determination to complete her mission.

He wished he had been conscious when she left. He wished he could have measured her words as she explained her reasons for leaving. Despite what Nellie had told him, it was hard for him to believe she would give up like that. Luke was a pretty good judge of character and he could not believe that Caroline was such a weakling.

———

"It's likely to get pretty rough from here on, Caroline," Ben Nichols was saying. "Why don't you go on back? I'll get the message through and I'll bring your pa back to you."

"I'm not going to quit," Caroline said. She took a drink of water, then handed the canteen back to Ben. Ben put the cork in and hung it on his saddle pommel.

"That's a good girl," Ben said.

"Ben?"

"Yes?" Ben swung back into his saddle.

"Ben, do you think the men of the Alamo will leave?"

"No, I don't."

"Even though they are being ordered to leave by General Houston?"

"This isn't the first time Houston has told 'em to leave," Ben said. "He wrote a letter explaining all about his strategy for winning this war. We're supposed to form a cavalry to ride all over Texas, keeping our forces together and striking against the long supply lines of the Mexican Army."

"Is that a good plan?"

"It's an outstanding plan," Ben admitted. "And it's the plan that's going to win this war. But that won't do the defenders of the Alamo any good, no matter what Sam Houston says."

"But why not? I don't understand," Caroline said.

"Well, I reckon it's a matter of pride as much as anything else," Ben said. "You see, Neill, Crockett, Bowie, your pa, and the others, they got it in their minds that no bunch of Mexicans are gonna run them out of the Alamo. They figure it would be yellow to leave."

"But you said yourself that a retreat would be logical," Caroline said.

"Logic's got nothing to do with pride," Ben said, "and the thing that's gonna keep all the Texans there is pride. It'll keep us there, too."

"Us?" Caroline asked weakly.

Ben twisted in his saddle and looked back over his shoulder at Caroline.

"Yeah," he said. "Us. Suppose we go there and deliver Sam Houston's message to the men and suppose they decide they ain't gonna leave? What are we gonna do? Do we just run like rabbits or do we stay there and fight with the defenders?"

"I—I don't know," Caroline said. "I guess I haven't given it much thought."

"Well, girl, you got about one day to think about it," Ben said dryly.

"One day?"

"Yeah. If we make it through the Mex Army, we'll be in San Antonio by this time tomorrow."

Chapter 10

Caroline held the horses while Ben stood at the top of a hill, peering through a spyglass at the valley before them. After several long moments, he came back down, collapsing the glass and putting it back into his saddlebag.

"Looks to me like every soldier in the Mexican Army is out there," he said.

"Can we get through?" Caroline asked anxiously.

"No way we can get through them," Ben said, "but we might be able to go around them."

"How long will that take?"

"Maybe as much as a week," Ben said. "We have to go way north."

"A week! We'll be too late."

"No, we won't," Ben said. "Old Santa Anna's got us outnumbered fifty to one but he's not taking any chances. He's going to wait until everything is exactly the way he wants it before he makes his move." Ben smiled. "Looks like you're goin' to have to put up with Ben Nichols for another week. That's fine with me. I enjoy the company of a pretty woman. But it sure can't be no bargain for you."

"Mr. Nichols, you have been the perfect gentle-man," Caroline said. "Your company has been very pleasant."

Ben laughed. "If I were a few years' younger lass, I'd make my move, you can be sure of that."

Ben set a northward course and he and Caroline rode hard, always keeping a line of hills or trees or rocks between them and the thousands of Mexican soldiers who were in the area.

One didn't have to be a scout to sense the presence of the Mexican soldiers. At night, the low-hanging clouds glowed red with the light of their campfires and, by day, the dust cloud raised by their horses rose high into the heavens.

Three days later, Ben Nichols and Caroline were far enough north to start working their way south again and it was during their turnabout that they encoun-tered half a dozen wagons in an encampment. Caro-line recognized Reuben Butcher, the wagon master she had met at the settlement.

"Mr. Butcher!" she said, smiling as if seeing an old friend though she had met him only briefly. "What are you doing here? I thought you weren't going to lead this wagon train."

Reuben greeted Caroline and Ben. "I didn't intend to," he said. "But these damn fools were so set on coming that they doubled my money. I would've been branded a coward if I'd refused, now, wouldn't I?"

"How has it gone?" Ben asked.

"We've run into quite a few Mex troops," Reuben said. "The civilized ones just searched our wagons to make sure we weren't carryin' a load of weapons, then let us go on through. Then we ran across a bunch of Texans that I wished the Mexicans would get hold of. They called themselves the Texas Warriors and they tried to pass themselves off as irregulars but they were nothin' but a bunch of thieves. They stole half of our provisions and took what gold they could find. They called it military confiscation. Confiscation be damned. It was out 'n' out thievery."

"There are quite a few outlaws, takin' advantage of the situation right now," Ben agreed. "But once we get this war won, we'll go after them. We'll settle their hash—you can count on that. Who were they, do you know?"

"I don't have any idea," Reuben said. "The leader was a big, ugly fella, I know that. He had green eyes, like a coyote, and he had a big, puffed-up scar on his cheek in the shape of a cross."

"He'll pay his dues one day soon," Ben said.

Ben and Caroline joined Reuben at his campfire and drank coffee as they talked. Reuben poured himself a second cup. "Say, I reckon you heard about Luke Calhoun, didn't you?"

Caroline had told Ben Nichols about Luke during their days together and Ben looked over toward her as soon as Reuben mentioned Luke's name. Caroline was looking at Reuben anxiously.

"I'm not sure," Ben said. "What are you talkin' about?"

"Luke got himself killed," Reuben said casually.

"What?" Caroline asked with a gasping intake of breath. Reuben looked at her curiously.

"But how was he killed? Where?" Caroline stammered. Reuben showed some concern over Caroline's reaction. He put his cup down and went over to put his hand on her shoulder.

"Girl, I'm sorry I blurted it out like I done," he said. "I didn't know it would upset you."

"Colonel Calhoun was Miss Lafont's guide before she hired me," Ben explained. "They became friends."

"I see," Reuben said. He was obviously trying to measure the weight of the word *friends,* not only as it pertained to Caroline and Luke but also as it pertained to Caroline and Ben Nichols

"Please," Caroline said. "Tell me what you know."

"Well, it seems that Luke got in a gunfight in some saloon. The saloonkeeper's wife patched him up and, when he was near recovered, he left. He wasn't gone for more than a day when he was set upon by a Mex patrol. He put up a fight but he was killed. That's all I know," Reuben said.

Tears flooded Caroline's eyes and she put down her coffee cup and walked away from the others so they wouldn't see her cry.

If she hadn't left Luke, this wouldn't have happened. If only she had stayed with him until he was fully recovered.

Caroline had just about cried herself out when she felt rather than heard Ben approach her. He came up behind her and put his arms around her gently. She turned to him, taking comfort where she could, crying on his shoulder.

"I'm sorry, lass," Ben said.

Caroline and Ben spent that night in the circle of the wagons. Caroline's sleep was fitful and filled with dreams of Luke Calhoun. She mourned him the next day as they continued their circuitous ride toward the Alamo but, by the following night, she was numb. The sharp pain had settled into a dull ache, buried beneath her heart. The love that had blossomed for Luke had been a recent emotion, fresh with excitement and heavy with promise, but unproven by the test of time. And if what Ben Nichols said about the Alamo was true, then the chances were very good that she herself would be dead within a few days.

Caroline thought of that. Until she left Louisiana, she had seen death only when it occurred naturally and, even then, only at stately funerals. In the last few weeks, she had become almost hardened to sudden and violent death. It did not surprise her that Luke had been a victim of the violence that swept through this wild country. He was, after all, a part of Texas. And now, so was she. If death was to come to her at the Alamo, so be it.

Though Caroline thought she had put it out of her mind, the grief came back to her in her sleep, and she whimpered pitifully. Then, suddenly, she awoke to find herself in Ben's arms.

"Ssh, girl, ssh," Ben said softly, holding her close to comfort her. "It'll be all right. You'll see. The world will go on."

"Ben," Caroline said, her words muffled by his closeness. "Oh, Ben, forgive me for being such a baby."

"It isn't being a baby to mourn for someone you love, darlin'. For if that was the case, I've been a baby a few times myself."

THE MAN CAROLINE had mourned was in fact not dead. In a land without newspapers, and with only scattered pockets of civilization to tame the wild frontier, rumors took the place of news and fabrication often supplanted fact. Therefore, on the very night Caroline was grieving his passing, Luke Calhoun was in one of the many saloons along the trail.

A young, pretty bar maid came to his table to deliver the beer he had bought.

"Buy yourself a drink and join me," Ben said.

The girl smiled. "I'll be right back."

Luke and the young girl talked for a few minutes, then the young girl said, "She must be very beautiful."

"Who must be very beautiful?" Luke answered.

"The one you are thinking of."

Surprised by the perception of the young girl, he asked, "Why do you believe I was thinking of another?"

"Most men, when we are talking, are thinking only of me. Your words are kind and gentle but I know you are thinking of another."

"I'm sorry," Luke said.

"Don't be sorry. Who is she? An old sweetheart?"

"It never quite got that far," Luke said.

"Someone who disappointed you?"

"Yes, very much." Luke reached across the table to take the young girl's hand but, in doing so, he winced from the pain in his shoulder.

"Oh, are you all right?"

"I'm fine. I have a shoulder wound. It's beginning to heal now. About the only thing that will remain is the scar."

"I am sorry you were hurt," she said. The expression on her face changed. "There was one here last week who also had a scar. But I'm not sorry for him. Whoever gave him the scar must have had good cause. He is a cruel man and I hope he never comes back here again. It's funny, you know? His scar is shaped like a cross. It should be something else, a symbol of the devil, maybe, but not a cross."

"What's that? A cross, you say? Was it on his cheek, here?"

"Yes," the girl answered, surprised by his sudden interest.

"Did he have green eyes?"

"Yes," the girl said. "Green and evil-looking."

"Joiner," Luke said. "It was Joiner."

"You know him?"

"Yes, I know him."

"I like you," the girl said, "but I don't like your friend. If you ever come here again, please don't bring him with you."

"I assure you," Luke said, "Joiner is no friend of mine. Do you know where he went?"

"I think he was heading west," the girl said. "I heard them talking about going to a place called the Alamo."

"You say you heard *them?* Who was with him?"

"He was with some men who call themselves Texas Warriors. They are pretending to be with the army but I don't believe them."

"How long ago was he here?"

"A few days," the girl said. "If he isn't your friend, why are you so anxious to find him?"

"Because," Luke said, "I want to kill him."

Chapter 11

Knute Joiner squatted on his haunches and tossed another mesquite branch onto the fire. Beyond the flickering flames, shadows came and went as his men, one by one, took their turns with the young Mexican woman they had captured earlier in the day. Joiner, of course, had been first. It was his right as the colonel.

Joiner chuckled. He had appointed himself colonel, just as he had appointed himself captain when he first formed the group. He would have appointed himself colonel at the beginning but his ignorance of military rank was such that he thought a captain was higher than a colonel. Not until later on did he realize that a colonel was a higher rank. Of course, as his "command" had no official recognition, he could choose any rank he wanted. He had created his own army and designated the men in his army by whatever rank he chose. He was the only officer because he wasn't sure what rank the other officers would be and he didn't want to take the chance of appointing someone to a higher position than he held himself. His second-in-command, he made a sergeant.

Sergeant Glover walked over to him, buttoning up his pants. He had just left the young woman for the second time.

"She's passed out again," Glover said. "She's just layin' there. If you ask me, it ain't no fun takin' a woman that just lies there 'n don't hardly move."

Joiner rubbed his fingers along the scar on his cheek. "Yeah, well, that's better'n to have her fight like a wildcat." Joiner recalled the woman who had given him the scar and he remembered the unexpected fight she had put up. She had been Mexican, too, only she was married to an American. An American named Luke Calhoun. Calhoun had killed Joiner's partner and would have killed Joiner, too, if he hadn't escaped. Joiner was always on the lookout for Calhoun. There was no way Calhoun was ever going to sneak up on him.

"Anyway, I'm done with her. I told the men that was wantin' to go again to hold off until I talked to you. You wanna have another turn?" Glover asked.

"Naw," Joiner said. He rubbed his scar again. "I'm a colonel. I gotta take care of my men, you know what I mean? Let 'em have their fun. Besides, I need 'em to be in good spirits for what we got to do."

"I'll tell 'em," Glover said. He walked over to the group of men who stood around looking down at the young, whimpering woman. He said something to them but he spoke so quietly that Joiner couldn't hear him. The men grunted in satisfaction and Joiner saw one of them loosen his belt and drop his pants before he went down over the girl again. Glover laughed at something one of the men said, then walked back to Joiner.

"Joiner, I been thinkin'," he said.

"It's Colonel Joiner to you, Sergeant," Joiner corrected, "and you ain't supposed to think. That's my job."

"Maybe so, Colonel Joiner," Glover said, "but I been thinkin' nonetheless, 'n' I want to ask you somethin'."

"All right, what is it?"

"Tell me again 'bout this here Alamo. Why we goin' there? Ain't it true that the Mexicans is goin' to surround the place?"

"Yeah," Joiner said, "but we'll be in and out before they get there."

"Why? All you've said is we're goin' to the Alamo but you ain't said *why.*"

Joiner smiled. The scar on his cheek had destroyed some of the muscles of his face so that his smile had become twisted and distorted. "We goin' after the gold they got there."

"You really think they got gold?" Glover asked.

"Are you kiddin'? They got a ton of it," Joiner said.

"Where'd you hear they got gold?"

"I heard it in a saloon on the Brazos."

"Hell, Joiner, that's saloon talk," Glover said.

"Saloon talk, is it?" Joiner retorted. "Well, this here fella jus' happens to be in tight with ol' Sam Houston hisself 'n he knowed what he was talkin' about. 'Course, iffen you don't want nothin' to do with it, why, you can jus' leave right now 'n I'll take your share."

"No," Glover said quickly. "I'm willin' to listen to more about it. What did this here fella say?"

"He said that Travis collected gold from all over west Texas. He was plannin' on givin' it to Sam Houston to help raise the Texas Army. But Travis and the others with him won't leave the Alamo now. They feel like they's the only thing standin' between Santa Anna's army and the rest of Texas. Besides, they think if they run it'll look liken they turned coward 'n skedaddled."

"All right, so what good is that gold gonna do us?"

"Ain't you got no kinda brains at all?" Joiner asked disgustedly. "We're gonna ride into the Alamo just like we was soldiers sent from ol' Sam Houston hisself. We gonna tell 'em how proud Houston 'n all Texas is that they is gonna stan' their groun' and fight the Mexicans. Then we gonna tell 'em to give us all the gold they's holdin' so we can take it back to Houston. Once we get it, we gonna ride plumb on outa Texas 'n be rich men for the rest of our lives."

"You think Travis'll give the gold to us?" Glover asked.

"What choice will he have?" Joiner asked. "It's either give it to us or let Santa Anna have it. If we go in there actin' like we're fightin' for Texas, he'll give it to us."

Glover's eyes glowed with excitement in the flickering flames of the campfire.

"Whooeee!" he said. "Colonel Joiner, I got to tell you, that's the best idee I've ever heard. Tell me, how much gold you reckon they really is?"

"They's enough for you and me to get rich," Joiner said. He looked around at the rest of his men and lowered his voice. "Iffen we don' have to share it with the others."

"How we gonna keep from it?"

"I'm gonna give these men to Travis to help 'im defend the Alamo," Joiner said. "They'll either be kilt off or took prisoner. Either way, we'll be gone afore they's anythin' they kin do 'bout it."

"You know, Colonel Joiner," Glover said, giggling. "You are sure one smart sumbitch."

"Yeah," Joiner answered, smiling back at him. "Ain't I, though?"

You don't know how smart, Joiner thought. You're also goin' to stay at the Alamo with the others.

"Hey! Anybody else want to take their turn with this here Mex girl?" a voice called from the night. "Anybody left who ain't had their turn yet?"

"Sounds like ever'one is finished with her," Glover said. "You want me to shoot her?"

Joiner looked toward the small lump on the ground which was the young woman. She had been riding in a wagon with an older man who they learned was her father.

They had shot the man who was with her, immediately, because Joiner wanted the woman for his men. At least, he told himself that he wanted the woman for his men, though he had been quick to claim his rightful place at the head of the line.

Such diversions helped to keep his men in good spirits, he knew, and he would have to keep them happy if he expected them to work their way through the Mexican lines and into the Alamo with him.

"You ain't answered, Colonel," Glover said. "What

do you want to do with the woman? You want me to shoot her?"

"No," Joiner said, feeling magnanimous. "Give her her clothes back and send her on her way."

"She'll be alive to tell what we done," Glover suggested.

"What the hell difference does it make?" Joiner asked. "What's she gonna say? That she was raped by an army? And who's she gonna tell? Just let her go. We might run across her again sometime 'n want the same thing."

Glover giggled. "Yeah," he said. "Yeah, you're right."

Dumb, Joiner thought. All his men were dumb. He sighed. Maybe that's what you had to put up with when you were the commanding officer.

Joiner stood up and walked a few paces away from the fire to the blanket he had spread out for himself. He took off his boots and used them for a pillow. He heard the soft, whimpering voice of the young woman as Glover talked to her, then he saw her get up, slowly, painfully, heavily, and limp off into the darkness. Maybe he should have killed her, he thought. She would probably die out there anyway. Well, that was her problem. He had to get some sleep. It would be a long, hard ride to reach the Alamo before it came under attack.

———

AT FIRST, Luke thought it was just the movement of a bit of shrubbery. It was a clump of black against the ground but it moved in a jerky, irregular pattern, though it did, at times, seem to move against the wind. Then, as he rode closer, he saw that it wasn't shrubbery at all. It was a person walking. *Walking* wasn't actually the word for it, however. The person was doing a lot more falling and stumbling than walking. And, Luke saw, it was a young woman.

Luke put his horse into a canter and rode toward the stumbling figure. He dismounted when he reached her and held out his canteen. As she looked up at him with a face disfigured by bruises and swelling, he drew in his breath quickly. This was Maria Romero, the daughter of Adriana's brother. This was Luke's niece!

"Maria!" Luke said. "Maria! What happened? Who did this to you?"

Maria looked into Luke's face and her bruised features managed to twist into a smile.

"Uncle," she said softly. "Uncle, some bad men, they— they—"

"Never mind," Luke said. He scooped her up gently into his arms and carried her to his horse. He put her up, then got on behind her. It was a two-day ride to the Romero ranch but he meant to take her there.

During the first night, Maria was delirious. She whimpered all night and, though it wasn't exceptionally cold, Luke built a fire and wrapped her in his blanket. She was so young and helpless that his heart filled with pity for her and his mind grew cold with hate for the men who would do such a thing.

The chill that had come in the night had passed by the next morning but the anguish lingered on. Luke tried to talk to Maria, to get her to tell him what happened, but she could say nothing. A few times she tried to speak but the words died in her throat and her eyes flooded with tears.

"Don't worry, my little one," Luke said. She was riding on the saddle in front of him and he put his arm around her and comforted her as he would a child.

Toward evening of the second day, he reached the Romero ranch. Two armed men rode out to challenge him but when they saw who it was, they smiled and put their rifles away and came to greet him. The smiles left their faces when they saw the granddaughter of their patron.

"I found her on the trail," Luke said.

One of the two guards rode off at a gallop to spread the news. By the time Luke arrived at the main house, there were two dozen people standing outside to help with Maria. They carried her gently inside and put her to bed. Then the men took care of Luke's horse while he went inside for supper.

During the meal, Luke told Don Pedro Romero how he had found Maria, explaining to her worried grandfather that she had been unable to talk to him. They caught up on the events that had occurred since their last meeting and they discussed the war. Don Pedro Romero had known that Luke was a colonel in the Texas Militia and he hadn't questioned it. He had declared himself a neutral, however, because he would have to live here after the war, no matter who won.

"There is good and bad on both sides," he had said. "I will rejoice in the good and reject the bad, whichever side wins."

After supper, Luke went into the parlor where he was served a drink made from tequila. Word was sent to Romero that Maria was asking for him and everyone was brightened by the news that she was able to talk again. Luke waited in the parlor while Don Pedro went to his granddaughter.

"She told me my son was killed by the same men who did this to her," Don Pedro said as he came from her bedroom a while later and sat down next to Luke, his face lined with grief.

"Were they Americans?" Luke asked.

"They were evil," Romero said. "Evil does not recognize boundaries."

"Were they Americans?" Luke asked again.

"*Sí*," Romero said. He sighed and reached out to let his hand rest on Luke's shoulder. "My son, it grieves me to tell you this but the men were led by the same one you seek—the man who killed my daughter, your wife."

"Joiner?" Luke asked. "Joiner did this to Maria?"

"Joiner, *sí*," Romero said. "The one with the *cruz* on his cheek."

"When I find him," Luke promised, "I shall carve a cross on his heart."

Chapter 12

"Caroline, it is time to be awake," Ben said quietly. Caroline opened her eyes and looked up into Ben's face.

"Oh, Ben," Caroline said, sitting up and seeing that it was daylight, "you let me oversleep. We should have been on our way long ago."

"No need, lass," Ben said gently. "We're only a few miles from San Antonio. We'll reach the Alamo today. I've made coffee."

"Umm, thank you," Caroline said.

———

THE INSIDE of the tent was lined with red, green, and white satin. A canvas floor covering was stretched over the level ground and an ornate Persian rug was spread over the canvas.

In the middle of the tent stood a table that would have been at home in the finest dining room in Mexico City. It was set with silver, crystal, and china that sparkled in rich array. A roast suckling pig, gleaming in a golden-brown glaze, occupied the position of honor at the center of the table, surrounded by plates of vegetables and fruits.

This was the field headquarters of General Santa Anna. As military dictator of all of Mexico, he had used his power to build the greatest army in the history of Mexico and now he was taking that army to Texas to crush the upstart Americans who had had the temerity to rebel against him. He would be ruthless in his prosecution of the war against them. The only way to end the rebellion would be to wipe the Americans out entirely and if that meant killing every Texan who opposed him, then that was what he would do.

General Santa Anna did not believe in permitting the rigors of field duty to interfere with his love of luxury, however. He was in an enviable position because he could enjoy all the luxury he craved simply by ordering that his wishes be carried out. Six coaches and wagons accompanied him wherever he went. They carried all the accoutrements of luxurious living: silken sheets, gold and silver ornaments, rugs, china, crystal, elegant uniforms, and such furniture as he required to be comfortable.

That afternoon, General Santa Anna had conducted a grand review of the more than four thousand troops in his command. It had been a glorious spectacle, with the music of a dozen bands blaring and with scores of red, white, and green Mexican flags flapping in the breeze. The commanders of Santa Anna's troops had led the review, mounted on splendid horses, elegantly attired in scarlet and blue while behind them infantry-men, dressed in white uniforms and tall hats, marched in precise formation. Behind them rode the cavalry-men, holding their beribboned lances at high port, sitting tall in their saddles, their highly polished metal breastplates gleaming brilliantly in the sun.

General Santa Anna accepted their salutes with the assurance of a man who was confident of ultimate victory.

In a way, Santa Anna felt like a cat playing with a mouse. He had been within sight of the Alamo for several days now and, through his spyglass, he had observed the Texans scurrying about, trying to fortify the mission grounds by closing up gaps in the wall and moving cannon into position. It was a useless endeavor Santa Anna knew but he grudgingly admired the Texans for trying.

One thing puzzled Santa Anna. The Texans had known of his coming for several weeks. They had had plenty of opportunity to leave the garrison and join up with other Texans. Instead, they had chosen to remain. There couldn't be two hundred of them in that little mission. Why had they chosen to stay and fight against four thousand of the best-equipped and best-trained troops in the world?

Maybe they thought he would just pass them by. Perhaps they hoped they could remain there, forever a thorn in his side. Well, if that is what they were counting on, they were wrong. Santa Anna's very first order of business would be to take back the Alamo.

The loss of the Alamo by his brother-in-law, General Martin Perfecto de Cos, had been a slap in the face not only of the government of Mexico but of the family as well.

Santa Anna ate a piece of the roast pig. He was

licking the grease from his fingers when a soldier reported to him.

"Excellency, there is an officer outside who wishes an audience with you."

"An audience about what?"

"I don't know, Excellency," the messenger replied.

"Send him away," Santa Anna said with an impatient wave of his hand.

"He says he is a relative of yours, Excellency."

"What? Another relative?" Santa Anna sighed. "The bane of the powerful is their relatives. Very well, show him in."

Santa Anna held his wine goblet out to be filled and the dark red wine had just been poured when the visitor came in. The general looked at him, then he smiled.

"So, Don Esteban Juan Lopez," he said, "we meet again." Santa Anna looked at Lopez's uniform. "I see you have managed to keep your commission. What are you now?"

"I am a captain, Your Excellency."

"A captain?" Santa Anna said. He shook his head and clucked sadly. "Surely you would have been a general by now had it not been for your indiscretion. Where is the other fool? What was his name? Gonzara? The one you persuaded to take the responsibility for your indiscretion?"

"As I took the responsibility for yours, Excellency?"

Santa Anna laughed. "Ah, yes, I do recall now. It was I who dallied with the wife of the minister of the treasury, wasn't it? And you did accept the blame, I believe."

"In return for your sparing my father from execution," Lopez said.

"Yes, well, you will be pleased to hear that your father is living happily in his own home, none the worse for his attempted rebellion."

"It wasn't a rebellion, General. He merely stood for election."

"Against my wishes," Santa Anna said. "I considered that treason. Well, enough of that. Where is Gonzara?"

"Gonzara is dead, Your Excellency."

"Dead? What a shame," he said in a voice that expressed no feeling at all. "What happened?"

"My men caught him spying for the Texans."

"Oh? So, you thought to put love of your country above your personal debt to Gonzara, is that it?"

"Yes, Your Excellency."

"Such devotion to duty should be rewarded." Santa Anna waved his hand. "I hereby restore you to your rank of colonel."

"Thank you, Excellency," Lopez said.

Santa Anna reached for another piece of roast pork but saw that Lopez had made no attempt to leave.

"Is there something else?"

"Yes, Your Excellency," Lopez said. "My men fought an engagement with a Texas company led by a man named Lieutenant McAfee. McAfee was killed but I found a message he was carrying from Sam Houston to Colonel James Neill, commander of the Texas Garrison inside the Alamo."

"Oh? And what did that message say?"

"It commanded the colonel and his men to abandon the Alamo. Evidently, the message had been sent twice before, once by Jim Bowie and once by Luke Calhoun. Bowie reached the Alamo and joined with the rebels and Calhoun was evidently killed."

"And you killed McAfee."

"Yes. General, I have a proposal. Let me go to the Alamo under a white flag. I will tell Neill of his commander's wishes. Perhaps I can convince him to surrender the Alamo without a fight."

"Without a fight?" Santa Anna said, frowning at Lopez. "Why on earth would I want to do that?"

"I thought it might prevent bloodshed, General."

Santa Anna laughed. "I have news for you, Colonel. The Alamo is no longer under the command of Colonel Neill. Instead, my informants tell me, there is a sort of dual command exercised by Jim Bowie and Colonel William Travis."

"Jim Bowie I know," Lopez said. "But what of this Travis? Who is he?"

"His name is William Barret Travis," Santa Anna said. "He is an incurable romantic who believes himself destined for fame or an early death. He was born in South Carolina and he married a woman in Alabama. His wife took a lover. Colonel Travis killed the lover and came to Texas."

"You seem to know a great deal about him," Lopez said.

"It is the duty of a commander to understand his enemy," Santa Anna said.

"Where is Colonel Neill?"

"Gone," Santa Anna said. "He claimed that there was illness in his family but it is my belief that he has no stomach for the fight that is to come."

"Then I am certain we can talk the rest of the

defenders into abandoning San Antonio to us," Lopez suggested.

"I have no intention of letting them surrender without a fight," Santa Anna said. "I am going to crush them, completely and ruthlessly. When news of my victory over the defenders of the Alamo travels around Texas, when the other so-called citizen soldiers hear what fate awaits those who dare to challenge my power and authority, this rebellion will end. No, my dear cousin, there will be no flag of truce and you will not deliver Houston's message. I am going to crush the Americans once and for all."

"When?" Lopez asked. "General, you have the Texans outnumbered forty to one now. When are you going to attack?"

"At my own convenience, Colonel," Santa Anna answered. "At my own convenience." He smiled broadly. "But enough of this. Have you seen the young ladies we persuaded to join our expedition?"

"No, I haven't, Your Excellency," Lopez said.

"Ah, well, you shall," Santa Anna said.

———

"How are you, little one?" Luke asked Maria. The sun was splashing bright and yellow through the window of Maria's room and the young girl had been staring at the birds in the tree outside. She turned her head toward Luke and he could see the bruises on her face though, mercifully, the swelling had gone down.

"Uncle, why did those men do such things?" Maria asked in a small, hurt voice.

Luke sat on the edge of the bed and took Maria's small hand in his.

"Some men aren't fit to live with decent people and they should be killed. The men who did this to you are such people."

"It was terrible," Maria said. Tears slid down her cheeks.

"I know it was," Luke said. He leaned over and softly kissed each tear in its track. Maria put her arms around him and squeezed him tightly, pulling him to her. After a long moment, she released him and Luke straightened up.

"Maria," he said, "do you remember hearing them say anything that might help me find them?"

"No," Maria said. "They spoke, only about me. They said awful things and they laughed when they hurt me."

Luke was disappointed that she wasn't able to tell him anything to help him. He brushed her hair gently back from her forehead. "I'll find them. I promise you, I'll find them."

Luke kissed her forehead, then he stood up and started to leave.

"Trees," Maria said.

Luke stopped and looked toward her, "Trees?"

"I heard them say something about going to a group of trees—*alamo* trees."

"The Alamo?" Luke said excitedly. "Are they going to the Alamo?"

"What is that?"

"It's a mission that has been turned into a fort," Luke said. "It is called the Alamo after a stand of *alamo* trees that grow nearby. Maria, is that where they are going?"

"Yes," Maria said.

"I don't understand," Luke said. "There are only brave soldiers at the Alamo and they may all die. Why would men like that go to the Alamo?"

"They said something about gold," Maria said. "They are going there for gold."

"Ha!" Luke said, slamming his fist into his hand. "Yes, they would do that! They have heard the rumor that Colonel Neill has gold there to buy weapons. They would go there if they thought there was some way they could get it."

"Is there gold there, Uncle?"

"No," Luke said. "I have read Colonel Neill's letters to Sam Houston. According to Neill, there isn't one dollar there. Joiner and his men are riding into a trap."

"I hope they are all killed in the trap," Maria said.

"I don't," Luke said.

Maria looked surprised at her uncle's statement. "Why not?"

"For two reasons," Luke said. "One is they don't have the right to die with brave men. The other is that I want Joiner for myself. I want him to know that I have found him."

"You will find him, Uncle," Maria said confidently. "I know you will."

Luke smiled at his niece. Then he left her room and returned to the parlor, where his father-in-law was waiting for him.

"She is better this morning," Luke said.

"She is young and strong and that is to her advantage," Don Pedro said.

"Yes," Luke agreed. "She said that Joiner and the others are headed for the Alamo."

"But why?" Romero asked as surprised as Luke had been by this information. "The defenders of the Alamo will all die."

"Yes," Luke said. "You can believe that Joiner doesn't intend to stay and help with its defense. Maria said his men spoke of gold."

"Is there gold at the Alamo?"

"No, there isn't," Luke said. "But there was a rumor that Colonel Neill had gathered some gold with which to buy weapons."

"Are you certain the story is false?"

"Absolutely certain," Luke said. He smiled. "But I am glad Joiner believed it. Now I know where to find him."

Romero put his hand on Luke's shoulder. "My son, if you go to the Alamo, the fate that awaits the others will be yours as well."

"Yes," Luke said. "This I know."

"Then why go?"

"I want to find Joiner," Luke said. "It is worth giving up my life to find him."

"But if he gets caught in the Alamo, he will die anyway. There's no need for you to go."

"If there's any way to escape, Joiner will find it," Luke said. "I don't intend to let him escape. Besides, it is as I told Maria. Joiner does not deserve to die with brave men. He must die alone like the coward he is and he must know why he is dying."

"You are doing this for my daughter and my granddaughter?"

"And your son," Luke replied.

Romero shook his head. "No, I think now you are doing this for yourself, Luke. You have a thirst for revenge that can be slaked only by blood."

"Perhaps that is correct," Luke admitted. "I know only this. I will find Joiner. If I have to follow him into the depths of hell, I will find him and I will have my revenge, even if it be on the devil's doorsteps."

Don Pedro Romero crossed himself.

"I'm sorry, Don Pedro," Luke said. "I had no wish to offend you."

"I am not offended," Romero said. "I am worried about your offense before God."

"Pray for me, Don Pedro."

"I will pray for you," Romero said. "But I will do something more. If you must go after this evil man, I have a *pistola* I want you to use."

"I am accustomed to my own pistol," Luke began but Romero held up his hand to interrupt him.

"This is a most marvelous *pistola.*" Romero said. "How many times will your gun shoot?"

"Once, just like all other pistols," Luke said.

Romero smiled and opened a wooden case. The case was lined with red felt and in it was a pistol unlike any Luke had ever seen. He picked it up and looked at it. There was a strange cylinder between the barrel and the grip.

"This is called a revolver," Romero explained. "You can prepare up to six paper cartridges in advance, load them and the ball into the chambers of this cylinder. Then you will be able to fire six shots without reloading. The chambers of the cylinder line up with the barrel and, when you pull the trigger, the cylinder rotates and the next chamber lines up."

"I have never heard of such a weapon," Luke said in admiration.

"It will give you an advantage, will it not?"

Luke hefted the pistol, then aimed it at a twig outside the window. The balance was as good as, if not better than, that of the pistol he was now carrying.

"An advantage?" Luke said. "It will make me invulnerable."

Chapter 13

The town of San Antonio de Béxar was bordered by San Pedro Creek to the west and a horseshoe bend in the San Antonio River to the east. About four hundred yards of rolling terrain lay between the Alamo and a footbridge that crossed the river at the east end of the town.

When Caroline and Ben rode into San Antonio, they were immediately besieged with questions by people from the town as well as from the fort.

"Is there fighting anywhere else?"

"Do the others know we intend to make a stand here?"

"Have you seen any Mexican soldiers?"

"Do you know where Santa Anna is?"

Ben answered all of the questions, including the one about Santa Anna. He knew he wasn't telling them anything new but was merely satisfying their eagerness to talk to someone from outside.

"Santa Anna is on his way, I'm afraid," Ben said.

"Let 'im come," one of the Alamo defenders said. "We're ready for him."

"Is my father inside the fort?" Caroline asked.

"Her father is Henri Lafont," Ben explained.

"Henri? Yes, you'll find him there. He and Green Jameson and Almeron Dickinson have pretty nigh built the Alamo defenses single-handed. Wait till you see how they got the place fortified. Why, I'll jus' bet we could stand off ten thousand Mexicans iffen we had to."

"You may have to," Ben said ominously.

"Ben, let's hurry," Caroline said. "I want to see my father."

"I don't blame you for that, Caroline. You've come all this way and you got a right to be anxious. Come on, we'll go find him."

Caroline followed Ben through the streets of San Antonio, across the San Antonio River and up to a large walled enclosure that spread out over three acres.

"I had no idea it was so big," Caroline exclaimed as they approached the bastion.

"Yes," Ben said. "And there lies the rub. We've less than two hundred men to defend a wall that stretches more than a quarter of a mile. That's scarcely enough."

Ben and Caroline reached a small irrigation ditch that ran alongside the wall and they rode parallel to it until they came to the south gate. A tall, lean Texan was standing near the wall just outside the gate. His rifle was propped up beside him, and he was smoking a thin pipe.

"Ben?" The soldier said with a grin. "I figured

you'd have enough sense to stay gone once you'd left here."

"I reckon not," Ben answered easily. "How are you, Noah?"

"Got no complaints. You heard 'bout Colonel Neill leavin', didn't you?"

"No."

"He took off on a leave, said they was illness in his family."

"Then it must be true," Ben said. "Colonel Neill is no coward."

"No, I reckon not," Noah said. "Does make a man wonder though. Who's the lady?"

Ben smiled. "This is Henri's daughter, Caroline."

"Miss Caroline, I'm right pleased to meet you, ma'am," Noah said with a polite touch to the brim of his hat. "Truth is, though, this warn't no place for you to come. Things is gonna go bad here, soon."

"I know," Caroline said.

"We want to see her father and Jim Bowie," Ben said. "Are they both inside?"

"Yep. You'll find Henri back there on the southwest corner. He's helpin' to put in the eighteen-pounder. Bowie is most likely in his room in the low barracks," Noah said with a jerk of his thumb toward a building that stood right up against the wall just behind him. "Bowie's been ailin' lately."

"Thanks, Noah."

Caroline followed Ben through the gate. Inside the wall, she saw a long, open area known as the plaza. A well stood in the middle of the area near a small gun emplacement with two cannons. More than a dozen men were working in the plaza and, as she and Ben dismounted, she heard one of them call her father's name.

"Hey, Major Lafont, where are we goin' to put the twelve-pounders?"

"On the east wall," a voice answered and Caroline felt a thrill as she heard her father's voice for the first time in more than a year. The sound was comfortable, familiar and heartwarming. "We've built a ramp just forward of the altar. Pull the guns up that ramp and put them on the parapet there. They'll defend the eastern approach."

"Yes, sir," the man answered.

Caroline looked toward the sound of her father's voice and saw him coming down a ramp from the corner. He looked leaner than she remembered but that wasn't the only change. He also looked—and there was no other way to put it—heroic.

Henri looked their way and when he saw Ben, he smiled. "Ben? What are you doing back here? I thought—" Henri stopped in midsentence and stared hard at Caroline. "No," he said quietly. He put his hand to his forehead. "No—I must be seeing things."

"You aren't seeing things, Father," Caroline said. "I'm really here."

"Caroline!" Henri shouted and he and Caroline ran toward each other with open arms. They embraced and kissed, then embraced again. They both began talking at the same time, then they laughed, and, finally, they were both crying.

"Let's go to my quarters," Henri finally said. "It wouldn't do for the men to see their operations major crying, now, would it?"

"I don't care who sees us," Caroline said. "I am so happy it doesn't matter."

A few moments later, Caroline, Ben, and her father were sitting in Henri's small room in the officers' quarters along the west wall. Henri took a bottle from his trunk and pulled the cork with a hollow-sounding pop.

"This is cognac," he said. "I've had this bottle with me ever since I left home."

He found two glasses and a cup, poured the liquor, then passed it to Caroline and Ben. He held the cup under his nose, sniffed the bouquet, then drank.

"Ah," he said. "I had nearly forgotten how good cognac tastes. And I had nearly forgotten how beautiful you are," he said to Caroline. "But tell me, my little one, what are you doing out here? Why aren't you at home with your mother and your sisters?"

"Because soon we will have no home," Caroline said.

"Oh? Why is this? Have you had some disaster? Has there been a hurricane? What has caused such a reversal?"

"There has been no hurricane, Father," Caroline said. "There is only Frank Sweeny."

"Frank Sweeny? What about him?"

"Father, you may remember that you and Frank Sweeny once made a contract leaving all your worldly possessions to each other in the event that one of you should die," Caroline said. "Well, there has been no word from you since you left and Frank has gone to court to have you declared legally dead. As soon as the court does so—our land, the house, everything will belong to him."

"What? Why, that's preposterous!" Henri sputtered. "In the first place, that agreement was made many years ago when Frank and I were just starting the business together. Neither of us was married and neither of us had relatives to leave our holdings to, so we made that agreement between ourselves. It was his idea, at that. Anyway, the moment I married your mother, that agreement was abrogated and I drew up a new will."

"Where did you keep the new will?" Caroline asked.

"Why, safely in…" Henri stopped. "In my desk in the office in town," he said. "Which means …"

"That Frank Sweeny could have found it and destroyed it," Caroline finished quietly.

"Anyway, as you can plainly see, I am not dead, not yet anyway. So, there's no problem. Colonel Travis is a lawyer. I shall simply have him draw up a new will for me, and you can take it back to Louisiana. But I don't understand why Frank is trying to have me declared dead. I have written home at least once a week ever since I left."

"Father, we have not heard one word from you."

The expression on Henri's face grew sad and he drew his daughter to him. He embraced her, brushed her hair back, and kissed her on the temple.

"I'm sorry, my darling," he said. "I can only blame that on the undependability of the mail."

"Or on the dishonesty of Frank Sweeny?"

"Or the dishonesty of Frank Sweeny," Henri agreed. "I have known of Frank's dishonesty for a long time. I thought my knowing about it would protect me from it. I can see that I was wrong."

"He is an evil man, Father," Caroline said.

"Well, never you mind," Henri said. He smiled broadly. "I have placed a letter in a safety box at the New Orleans National Bank. It will invalidate any claim Sweeny might make. Simply go to the bank and remove that letter. It sets forth the terms of my current will and it will free you from Frank Sweeny's perfidy."

"I'll let you remove the letter," Caroline said.

The smile remained on Henri's face but it saddened. "Caroline, I thought you knew."

"Knew what?"

"I won't be leavin' the Alamo alive. None of us will, except you and some of the other women. I expect you'll be leavin' tomorrow at the latest."

"Oh, Father, you don't mean that. If you don't leave, I won't leave."

"Henri, Caroline is carrying a message from Sam Houston," Ben said. "She is supposed to deliver it to Jim Bowie."

"Well, Jim is holed up over in his room," Henri said. "He's been runnin' a high fever and coughing a lot. There've been times when I didn't think he'd live long enough for Santa Anna's men to kill him. Come on, I'll take you to him."

They walked back outside and Caroline saw men lashing ladders to the wall of the officers' quarters.

"Why the ladders?" she asked.

"That's to give our riflemen a way to climb up to the roof," Henri said. He pointed to the top of the wall all the way around the fort. "We'll have rifles and cannon, as thick as we can. We won't be able to stop the Mexicans but we can make them pay dearly when they do decide to come."

It was difficult for Caroline to comprehend what was happening. Here they were in Texas, her father, Ben Nichols, and herself. The Mexicans were going to attack and they would all die. How could this be taking place?

They cut across at an angle from Henri's quarters on the west wall to Jim Bowie's quarters on the south wall. They went past a well and Henri scooped a dipperful of water from the bucket and took a drink.

"This is one thing in our favor," he said. "At least they can't cut us off from our supply of water."

They reached the building known as the low barracks and Henri knocked on a door.

"Jim, I've got a surprise visitor for you. Someone you haven't seen in a long time."

The door opened, there, looking out through deep-set eyes under heavy brows, was Jim Bowie. He had always been a big, muscular man, and he was still big, though Caroline could see he was weakened by the illness that plagued him.

The very name of Jim Bowie inspired fear. He had grown up in the bayous of Louisiana and, as a young man, he used to ride alligators just for fun.

The rough-and-tumble life Jim Bowie led caused him to come at odds with others and, early on, he had earned a reputation as a knife fighter. In one memorable encounter, Bowie was shot in the hip and shoulder, stabbed in the chest, and beaten on the head. Before he fell, however, he slashed one of his attackers to ribbons, disemboweled a second, and nearly beheaded a third. He felled the fourth with a well-thrown blade as the attacker tried to flee.

Jim Bowie had designed a knife so lethal that it was known as the Bowie knife.

Caroline could remember him in a more personal way, however. Once, while riding in a stage to New Orleans with Jim Bowie and her father, a rather obnoxious man had begun smoking a foul-smelling pipe. The motion of the stage and the smell of the pipe combined to make Caroline ill and she had asked, in a small voice, if the man would mind not smoking.

The man told her to mind her own business.

Jim Bowie put the point of his knife to the man's neck and asked the man if he didn't think he would be more comfortable walking the rest of the way to New Orleans. The man, with a frightened nod, agreed that the fresh air would do him good.

That memory came back to Caroline as she looked at the man who had been her father's friend for such a long time and, when Bowie smiled at her, she went into his arms. As they embraced, she could feel the heat of the fever that was burning in him.

"You are a sight for sore eyes, Caroline," Jim Bowie said. "But I have to say this is no place for you."

"Mr. Bowie, I have a message for you," Caroline said. "It's from Sam Houston."

"I think I know the message," Bowie said. "Houston wants us to pull out of the Alamo. He wants us to give it up without a fight."

"Yes," Caroline said. "He believes that you and your men will be of more service to Texas if you remain mobile. That's why—" Caroline suddenly stopped in midsentence. "You knew?"

"Yep. He's sent me the same message before. I'm going to ignore it now, just as I ignored it then."

Despite her affection for Jim Bowie, Caroline suddenly felt only an intense anger. Luke Calhoun had lost his life trying to deliver that message. She had risked hers and she would undoubtedly die with the defenders of the Alamo. And for what? Jim Bowie had already received the message and he refused to obey Houston's order.

"The fact is," Bowie went on, "I arrived here in January at the head of thirty men, for the sole purpose of helping in the evacuation. I was sent here by Houston, personally."

"Then why in heaven's name didn't you carry out his orders?" Caroline asked.

"I'll tell you why," Bowie said. "I don't know much about a grand plan to defend Texas but I do know about fighting. And I do know about men. This post is the only one between Santa Anna and the Sabine River. Why, to just give it up to the Mexicans would be almost criminal. They'll take it from us, make no mistake about that. But they are gonna pay one hell of a price for it. And all over Texas—hell, all over America—folks'll remember the Alamo and that memory will spur 'em on to fight better than they ever thought they could. The whole war may turn on what we do here. I know what the message is but I hope you can understand that I have no intention of following it."

"I ... I guess I do understand," Caroline said, disappointed and depressed.

"Good. Tomorrow when you leave you can take a message back to—"

"I'm not leaving tomorrow," Caroline said interrupting Bowie's declaration.

Surprised, Jim looked at Henri.

"Don't look at me," Henri said. "I've already spoken to her."

"You *are* leaving," Jim said resolutely. "I am the commanding officer of this garrison and you cannot stay here without my permission. I don't intend to give you that permission."

"Then you'll have to physically escort me off the premises, sir, for I intend to stay."

"Henri?" Jim asked.

"I've begged her to leave but to no avail."

Jim sighed. "Well, if her own pa can't get her to leave, then I don't reckon I can, either. I suppose you can stay."

"Oh, Mr. Bowie, thank you," Caroline said, throwing her arms around Jim Bowie's neck.

Chapter 14

Caroline, Ben, and Henri left Jim's room, and Henri took them on a tour of the fortifications he had helped build.

"As you can see," Henri explained, pointing as he talked, "we have built several platforms from wood and earth, to put into position alongside the twelve-foot-high walls. Back over here, between the low barracks and the church, there was a gap in the wall more than seventy-five feet long. We filled that up with heavy logs and dirt. We had to do the same thing over there on the eastern end of the north wall. We've put guns where we could, the one eighteen-pounder at the southwest corner, a battery of twelve-pounders on the east wall, and eight-pounders and the lighter guns at other key places."

"It looks like you've done a fine job, Henri," Ben said.

Henri scratched his chin and looked around. "I guess not too many men get the opportunity to design the place where they will die," he said, "but I'm proud enough of it."

"Tell me about Travis," Ben said. "How do he and Bowie get along?"

Henri smiled. "Not too well, I'm afraid. The colonel can't understand a man like Jim. Travis is too much of a book man, whereas Jim is a man's man. Oh, don't get me wrong, Travis is a fighter and I have confidence he'll make us all proud when he goes down. It's just that he and Bowie don't hit it off all that well."

"Which of them is in command?"

"They've got that worked out between them," Henri said.

"How?"

"Bowie is in command of all the volunteers and irregulars. Travis has the regulars."

"In an army like this, how does anyone know the difference between the two?" Ben asked.

"They don't," Henri said. "The fact that Jim is sick helps. Travis has just about taken over total command on a temporary basis until Jim gets to feeling better."

"And that'll be?"

"We won't live long enough to worry about it," Henri said. He pointed to the church. "Caroline, when the fighting starts, that's where I want you to be. We have about twenty-five women and children here. I'll want you with them."

"I'd prefer to stay with you," Caroline said.

"Look, I don't want you here at all," Henri said. "And if you have any respect for your father, you'll listen to what I say. When the fighting starts—you go to the church!"

"All right," Caroline agreed.

"I love you, Caroline."

"I love you, Father."

A relatively small man wearing a brown cassock scurried across the plaza in front of them. He had a bald spot on the crown of his head and what hair he had left was white.

"There's the padre," Henri said. Henri smiled broadly. "Honey, I'm going to introduce you to Susanna Dickinson. She's the wife of the chief engineer. I'm sure she will appreciate having another American woman for company."

Caroline stood at the door of the sacristy of the church which had been converted into a hospital. Two women were scrubbing the floors, while a third was rolling bandages. The one rolling the bandages was young, blond, and very pretty. She fit the description of Susanna Dickinson.

"Mrs. Dickinson?" Caroline called out softly.

The blonde turned toward Caroline's voice. When she saw that Caroline was a woman, she smiled warmly.

"My name is Susanna," she said.

"I'm Caroline Lafont."

"Oh, you must be Henri's daughter. Someone said you had arrived."

"Yes," Caroline said.

Susanna embraced her warmly, then brought her back into the hospital.

"Not exactly like a grand hospital in New Orleans, I suppose," she said. "But it is a hospital. And I suspect it will get its use."

"Do you intend to stay here when the Mexicans attack?" Caroline asked.

"Of course," Susanna said. "My husband is here. I am going to stay with him."

"I intend to stay, too," Caroline said.

"It's too bad you didn't arrive with a company of dragoons," Susanna said.

"What?"

"I was just teasing," Susanna said with a laugh. "We've sent half a dozen letters out, trying to get someone to come and help us, but as yet, no one has arrived. Maybe if we had some money to pay them ..."

"I've got almost a hundred and fifty dollars in gold," Caroline said, pointing to her vest. "The coins are sewed up inside this vest."

Susanna laughed. "What an ingenious method of hiding them," she said. "You actually have that much gold?"

Caroline nodded.

"Well, a hundred and fifty dollars won't hire an entire company of dragoons," Susanna said, "but it might buy us a little more powder. Why don't you give the money to Colonel Travis?"

"I will, gladly," Caroline said.

From out in the yard came the sound of a fiddle and bagpipes.

Susanna laughed. "There's Davy Crockett and that fool fiddle of his and Peter Donovan and his bagpipes. They've been holding contests ever since they arrived to see who's the best musician."

"Have they settled it?"

"Not who is the best," Susanna answered with a

laugh. "Though some of us have our opinion as to who is the loudest."

"Susanna why are you here?"

Susanna began to tell her own story.

"I was married when I was only fifteen," Susanna said. "That was seven years ago. Then my baby came along. If it hadn't been for this war, Almeron and I would be living a normal happy life with little Angelina. But one doesn't always get what one wants, I suppose. Or even what one expects. Take you, for example. Did you ever expect to find yourself in a mission in the middle of a war?"

"No," Caroline said. "In fact, until not long ago, I wanted only to find my father and save our home in Louisiana."

"Save your home," Susanna said wistfully. "Yes, I suppose that's what all of us are doing now."

The music had given birth to a celebration and the sounds of the celebration floated in through the window.

Caroline hurried over to look out the window.

"Susanna, Americans and Mexicans are celebrating together. Is it possible that soon they will be fighting one another?"

Susanna nodded grimly. "I can't explain what makes men so foolish," she said. "I gave up trying a long time ago."

———

AT DAWN, there was a great flurry of activity outside and when Caroline opened her eyes, she dressed quickly in a dress that Susanna had given her, and then she went to the door to look outside.

Many who had been staying in San Antonio de Béxar were now streaming into the fort. Carts full of belongings squeaked across the plaza and tall, solemn men walked beside somber-looking women. Caroline saw Ben Nichols coming toward her, smiling at her.

"Good morning," he said.

"Ben, what is it? What's going on?"

"Santa Anna has moved his army into an offensive position," he said, taking her hand. "Come with me, I'll show you."

Caroline climbed the ladder into the church belfry behind Ben, then looked through the long spyglass. She could see the flash of sunlight on the shiny breast-plates of the cavalrymen. An officer was galloping back and forth in front of them with his sword drawn. The Mexicans' uniforms were of bright red and blue and, though she realized that the formation might surely spell her doom, she had to admit that it was a beautiful and colorful sight.

"When will they attack?" Caroline asked.

"Soon," was all Ben could say. "Soon."

Refugees streamed in from San Antonio for the rest of the day. Then, toward evening, the gates were closed and barred.

Colonel Travis called a meeting of everyone inside the fort, and they all gathered in the plaza in front of the church.

"Good mornin', Miss Lafont," many of the men greeted, smiling warmly. Caroline had no idea who they were but she realized that, by now, all must be aware that Henri's daughter had arrived.

Colonel Travis began the meeting. He had sent two civilians, Smith and Sutherland, on a scouting mission. They had come so close to the Mexicans that they had been forced to flee at a gallop and Sutherland's horse had thrown him. Sutherland was on crutches now with a broken leg but he was there with the others.

"Gentlemen," he said, nodding toward Caroline, Susanna, and nearly a dozen other women, then added, "and ladies. I regret to inform you that our situation is critical. Though we have sent messages to Colonel Fannin at Goliad, he has refused our pleas for help. The only other town close enough to send reinforcements is Gonzales which is about sixty miles east of San Antonio. I will read you the message I have written to them."

Travis held his hand out toward a black man, his servant known only as Joe. Joe handed Travis the message.

Colonel Travis held up the message, cleared his throat, and began to read: "The enemy in large force is in sight. We want men and provisions. Send them to us. We have one hundred fifty men and are determined to defend the Alamo to the last. Give us assistance."

Travis looked at those assembled. "I am dispatching this message by Sutherland and Smith and I am sending a final message to Colonel Fannin. After that, we are on our own—and God help us all."

There was a buzz in response to his last statement but, after a short while, everyone quieted.

Davy Crockett spoke up then, his clear voice sounding unafraid and resolute. "Colonel, assign me to some place, and I and my Tennessee boys will defend it all right."

"Mr. Crockett, you have been a member of the United States Congress, sir, and yet you came here as a private. I would prefer to appoint you to a command."

"No, sir," Davy said. "I have come to aid you all that I can in your noble cause and all the honor I desire is that of defending the liberties of our common country."

Davy Crockett's words brought applause from the crowd and Colonel Travis walked over and put his hand on the frontiersman's shoulder. "All right, then to you shall go the honor of defending the place that is most vulnerable. I want you and your Tennesseans at the palisade between the church and the low barracks."

"Colonel?" Ben spoke up.

"Yes, Ben?"

"Colonel, it seems to me that Santa Anna could squeeze us out in a siege if he had a mind to...unless we did something about it."

"You have something in mind?"

"I thought I might take a handful of men outside the fort to search for food. Maybe we could round up some grain and some livestock."

"That's a good idea, Ben," Henri said. "As it is, we don't have enough food in here to feed this many people throughout a long siege."

"All right, take some volunteers and go out and find what you can," Travis suggested. "Jameson, Dickinson, cover them with your cannon."

"Cap'n I'll go with you," Joe said.

"I'm a captain?" Ben responded.

Travis smiled. "It would appear that Joe has just appointed you captain."

"Well, Sergeant Joe, I'd be glad to have you come with me."

"Yes, sir!" Joe replied with a big smile.

"Let's go, boys," Ben said and he and half a dozen others slipped out through the main gate to hunt for food.

"What about shells for our heavy cannon?" someone asked after Ben and the others were gone.

"We'll have to make do with what we have."

"We've got plenty of grapeshot," Jameson said. "We made it ourselves. Almeron here cut up all the horseshoes he could find. I tell you, that's gonna make some terrible kind of grapeshot. It'll cut the Mexicans down like a wheat scythe."

"Good," Travis said. "See that there is plenty of it near the guns. All right, men, we have a long day's work ahead. I suggest we get to it."

"Hurrah!" someone shouted. "Hurrah for Texas, boys, hurrah!"

Others joined in the cheer and the meeting broke up as the defenders took their positions.

"Miss Lafont, may I have a word with you?"

"Yes, of course," Caroline said, turning to face the young commander.

"I understand you have a hundred and fifty dollars' worth of gold coin."

"Yes," Caroline said. "I will gladly give it to you."

"No," Travis said. "It will do me no good, for my days are numbered."

"As are mine," Caroline reminded him.

"Maybe not."

"Colonel, I have already told you. I have no intention of leaving before the fight."

"I know and I have given up trying to persuade you to change your mind," Travis said. "But I will insist you stay in the church during the fighting. Perhaps you will survive that way."

"Perhaps," Caroline agreed without much conviction.

A short time later, much to Caroline's relief, Ben and the others returned to the fort, leading thirty head of cattle and hauling several bushels of corn in the cart being driven by Joe.

"Colonel Travis, sir, Cap'n Ben got us enough food for us 'n the animals to last for a long time."

"Probably longer than we will live," Travis said to Henri, who was standing with him.

Colonel Travis and Henri walked over to shake Ben's hand.

"Well done, Ben," Colonel Travis said. "You did well too, Joe. I'm proud of you."

"Why, thank you, sir," Joe replied with a proud smile.

"Colonel, they got their flag flyin' from the church belfry in town," Ben said.

"The tricolor?"

"No, sir, it's not the Mexican flag. It's a solid red banner."

"It's a signal," Travis explained grimly. "A red banner means no quarters for the enemy." Travis swallowed hard before he went on. "They intend to take no prisoners."

"The bastards," Henri said.

"They could be doing this just to unnerve us," Ben said.

"Well, let's give them our answer, shall we? Almeron?"

"Yes, sir," Almeron Dickinson answered.

"Throw them an eighteen-pound iron ball."

"Yes, sir!" Almeron said and, a moment later, the fort trembled under the firing of the eighteen-pound cannon.

There was no answering fire but, a few moments later, Caroline heard a bugle sounding the same call over and over again.

"What is the music?" Susanna asked.

"It is *El Degüello*," Travis said. "It means they will take no prisoners."

———

JIM BOWIE, who was still feverish and bedridden, wrote a message asking Santa Anna to agree to the same terms the Texans had imposed on the Mexicans when they took the Alamo in the first place—a surrender in which the Texans would be disarmed and allowed to return to their homes. Jameson agreed to carry the message to Santa Anna under a white flag.

Feeling resentful and angry, Caroline watched Jameson leave. If Bowie was willing to do this now, why had he been reluctant to do so before? A few days ago, the Texans could have left with honor. Now there would be only dishonor. She was certain that Santa Anna would refuse to comply— and she was right. A short while later, Jameson returned with a reply from an officer on Santa Anna's staff. The general was interested in nothing less than unconditional surrender.

Colonel Travis was angry that Bowie had offered to surrender. He would have taken action but, by now, the fever had overtaken Bowie and he lay on his cot nearly delirious. Travis called another meeting of his men.

"I have written yet again to the outside world," Travis said. "As it is a message from all of us, I want to share it with you, now."

Travis read his message to his troops: "To the people of Texas and all Americans in the world. Fellow citizens and compatriots, I am besieged by a thousand or more of the Mexicans under Santa Anna. The enemy has demanded a surrender at discretion, otherwise the garrison is to be put to the sword, if the fort is taken. I have answered the demand with a cannon shot and our flag still waves proudly from the walls. I shall never surrender or retreat. I call on you in the name of liberty, patriotism, and everything dear to the American character to come to our aid with all dispatch. The enemy is receiving reinforcements daily and will no doubt increase to three or four thousand in four or five days. If this call is neglected, I am determined to sustain myself as long as possible and die like a soldier who never forgets what is due to his own honor and that of his country. *Victory or death!*"

Travis literally shouted the last three words and his words were echoed again and again by the men of the Alamo.

Caroline felt tears streaking down her face but she didn't know if they were tears of fear, sorrow, or pride.

Chapter 15

Luke Calhoun stepped into the saloon and peered through the dim light that filtered in through the windows and door. He looked at the other patrons, studying each face closely before he stepped over to the bar. He wanted to make certain that Joiner wasn't lurking in the shadows.

Once Luke had satisfied himself that his quarry wasn't in the saloon, he moved over to the bar and ordered a drink.

"What news?" the saloon owner asked as he poured liquor in a glass. It was a common enough opening, for news traveled by word of mouth, conveyed by travelers passing through.

"None, I'm afraid," Luke said. "I've been a little out of touch with everything."

"Well, then," the barman said. "Perhaps I have news that will be of interest to you. You know of Santa Anna's siege of the Alamo?"

"Yes," Luke said. "I had hoped that McAfee would

get through in time to give them Houston's order to withdraw."

"Ah, you knew McAfee, then?"

"Knew him?"

"Yes. He's dead. He was killed by Mexican troops."

"No," Luke said, "I didn't know that. When did it happen?"

"About fifteen days ago," the barman said,

"No, it couldn't have been fifteen days ago," Luke said. If that had been so, it would not have been McAfee who passed through while he was wounded to take the message forward for him. That incident was but ten days ago.

"Yes, fifteen ... no, sixteen days ago," the bartender said.

Now Luke was confused. If McAfee had been killed sixteen days ago, how could Caroline have entrusted the message to him? Or had that story been a ruse? Could Caroline have gone on to the Alamo herself? *Surely not.*

"Did you hear of Colonel Travis's letter from the Alamo?" the barkeeper went on, eager to show that he was well informed.

"No," Luke said.

"It was a letter that would thrill any Texan," the saloonkeeper said. "It told of the danger they faced and of their determination to defend to the death the free soil of Texas."

"Brave words," Luke said, "but Texas would be better served if Travis and the others would abandon that place and keep themselves alive to fight elsewhere."

"I agree with you," the barman said. "But you have

to admire the courage and patriotism of the men, not only Travis but the others with him as well. Jim Bowie, Davy Crockett, Ben Nichols. Oh, say, here's a piece of news. The same rider who came through here with news of Travis's letter told us of a woman that came there. A girl by the name of Caroline Lafont. Her father is—"

"What?" Luke asked, his voice booming out the question so loudly that everyone in the saloon looked toward him. "What did you say the girl's name was?"

"Caroline Lafont. Her pa is there in the Alamo, and—"

"No!" Luke said. He put his hand on his forehead and squeezed, trying to squeeze out the pain of this moment. She hadn't gone back to Louisiana. She had gone on to the Alamo. She had tried to do his job for him. Why had she made such a decision? It was something Luke might never know for the chances of Caroline surviving the attack on the Alamo were slim indeed.

"Are you all right?" the bartender asked.

Slowly Luke took his hand down from his forehead. He wrapped it around the empty glass and the barman poured more liquor for him.

"Yeah," Luke finally said quietly, "I'm all right." Luke drank one more glass, then slid the glass back across the bar. "Do you want another?"

"No," Luke said. "If I am to reach the Alamo in time, I must keep my wits about me."

"Mister, did I hear you right? Did you say you are going to the Alamo?"

"Yes," Luke said.

"You are even crazier than Colonel Joiner."

Luke's eyes narrowed at the name and he looked right at the saloon owner. "What about Colonel Joiner?" he asked. Luke kept his voice calm so as not to give anything away. The barman might be a friend of Joiner's, so Luke didn't want to give any indication that he represented a threat to the green-eyed man. He didn't want Joiner warned.

"He and three of his men were through here day before yesterday," the saloon owner said. "They said they were going to help defend the Alamo. I asked him what he thought four people could do but he seemed to think he would be able to make some contribution."

"Did this Colonel Joiner have a scar on his cheek?" Luke asked. With one finger, he drew a cross on his cheek.

"Yeah, he had a scar, all right," the barman said. "Do you know him?"

"I know him."

"Well, if you are dead serious on going to the Alamo, you'll probably see him, 'cause I suspect he's there by now."

"Thanks," Luke said. He paid for the drinks. "I guess I'll just go look him up."

———

THE MEXICANS HAD ADVANCED to within artillery range of the Alamo and, for one week, they fired shot and shell into the fort. A few heavy iron balls hit the Texans' cannon, dismounting them, but not damaging them beyond repair. The barrage did some damage to the walls but the Texans were able to repair them quickly. Most of the cannonballs fell into the open plaza and, though the whistling and thudding were unnerving, no one was killed.

Caroline was in a constant state of fright for the first two days but she soon learned to endure the shelling with the same stoicism the others displayed. Then, on the first morning of March, she awoke to the news that help had arrived and she rushed out into the plaza to greet the new army.

There she discovered, not an army, but only four men. There was something about those men that made her uneasy. They looked at her with barely controlled lust and she wondered why no one else could see the evil behind their eyes. The man with the cross on his cheek, the one called Joiner, was the most sinister of the lot.

There was a whistling noise, then the crash of a heavy ball splitting the wooden platform of a parapet. The thunder of the cannon that had hurled the ball rolled across the open space. Sergeant Glover jumped. Then, with shaking hands, he turned up a bottle of whiskey and took a long swallow.

"Joiner, what is this?" he shouted, unnerved by the shelling. "You're goin' to get us kilt in here."

"Don't let the cannonade bother you none," Joiner said. "Travis allowed as to how there'd already been more'n two hundred balls hurled in here 'n no one has been hurt yet. Fact is, Travis's men is pickin' up what balls is still in good condition. They gonna use 'em for their own guns."

"Are you sure there's gold in here?" Glover asked. "I haven't seen any of it."

"Do you think they'd leave it out in the open?"

"I just know I want to get the gold and get outa here," Glover said shakily.

"We will. Don't worry about it."

"You say don't worry but ever'thin' else 'bout your plan has gone wrong. We was supposed to ride in here with more'n twenty men. Instead, when the men found out we was cornin' to the Alamo, all but two of 'em run. They's just four of us now."

"That's all right," Joiner said. "That means there's just two of 'em we'll have to deal with when we take the money and skedaddle."

"Swan and Mondell are good men, Joiner. They stayed with us after ever'one else lit out. What would it hurt to give 'em a share?"

"I don't intend to share anythin' with 'em," Joiner said.

"Suppose I give 'em some of my share?" Glover proposed.

Joiner smiled. "Sure, iffen it comes from your share, I got no complaints."

"Thanks," Glover said.

Another cannonball screamed into the fort and Glover let out a shout and ducked.

Joiner laughed. "While you are duckin' the shells, I'll go talk to Travis and find out where he's keepin' the gold."

Joiner found Colonel Travis with Jameson and some of the others at the parapet that had been damaged by the shell. Already, they were pulling out the split timbers, getting ready to replace them with new.

"Colonel Travis, sir, I would have a word with you," Joiner said, approaching Travis.

"Just a minute," Travis said, holding up his hand. "Almeron, do you think you could fashion an iron band to hold these braces together?"

"I think so, Colonel," Dickinson said, looking at the point indicated by Travis.

"Give it a try, will you?" Travis said. He brushed his hands together and walked away while the men worked industriously behind him. He gestured at Joiner, inviting him to come with him. "All this shelling, and not a man has been injured. But, every night, the Mexicans come closer with their guns and, before too long, they'll be pounding our walls down and there will be little we can do." Travis sighed. Though he was ostensibly speaking to Joiner, he was, in fact, thinking aloud.

"At least the spirits of my men are still high," he continued. "The Mexicans have killed none of us but we have killed many of them. I look to the Americans alone for aid. If it doesn't arrive soon, we'll just have to fight the Mexicans on their own terms."

"Have you sent out requests for aid?" Joiner asked.

"A dozen times or more," Travis answered.

"What about the gold?" Joiner asked.

Travis stopped walking and looked at Joiner with a bewildered expression.

"*What* gold?" he said.

"The gold you gathered for weapons," Joiner said. "Don't you think you should send it out 'stead of lettin' it fall into the hands of the Mexicans?"

Travis chuckled. "I wish I had some gold," he said. "Maybe I could have bought Colonel Fannin's services. Lord knows patriotism wasn't enough."

"You...you don't have no gold?" Joiner asked, stunned by Travis's statement.

"A few wedding rings," Travis said. "That's all you'll find around here. No, wait, Miss Lafont has some gold, I am told. About two hundred dollars' worth, I think."

"Two hundred dollars?" Joiner said.

"That's all the money you'll find in this place," Travis said. He caught sight of two men carrying a timber to the low barracks and he yelled at them. "No, men, that timber goes over here. Bring it to the eighteen-pounder!" Travis looked at Joiner. "You'll have to excuse me, Colonel," he said. "I must see to the repairs."

"Yes," Joiner said. "Go ahead." He watched Travis hurry away. So, there was only two hundred dollars here, was there? Well, that was better than nothing and he hadn't come this far to leave with nothing. Now all he had to do was find that money.

Ben Nichols was standing with Davy Crockett on the parapet above the church. At fifty years of age, Crockett was the oldest man in the bastion. Well known throughout America, he had served in Congress and had even been mentioned as a possible vice-presidential candidate. He carried a long rifle and he was such an expert marksman that he could snuff the flame from a candle at three hundred yards.

Davy finished loading his rifle and leaned back against the palisade, looking down at the Mexicans. They were about three hundred yards away, milling about in plain sight, aware that they were out of range of the Texans' rifles.

"Hey, now," Davy said. "Look at that fancy-dressed fella. He's got more geegaws and doodads than any of 'em. You reckon he's a general?"

"Which one?" Ben asked.

"That one standin' well back from the rest, leanin' on the wheel of that wagon."

"Yeah," Ben said, "I don't know if he's a general or not but he's got to be somebody high up. See how he's standin' back out of danger while the rest of 'em are up on the line?"

Davy chuckled. "He just *thinks* he's out of danger." Davy wet his finger and held it up to gauge the direction of the wind. Then he steadied the barrel of his rifle on the palisade and took careful aim. A moment later, smoke and fire belched from his roaring rifle and the recoil shook him. Ben kept his eyes on the distant figure Davy had pointed out. The Mexican officer suddenly grabbed his chest, staggered back against the side of the wagon, then slipped down.

"Got 'im," Davy said simply.

———

WHEN DON ESTEBAN LOPEZ saw Colonel Soldana fall, he let out a shocked gasp, then turned to look toward the walls of the Alamo, far in the distance. He saw a little puff of white smoke drifting away from the corner of the wall nearest the church.

"It is the tall one, the devil in the coonskin cap," someone said.

One of the sergeants gave Lopez his spyglass and Lopez looked toward the puff of smoke. He saw a tall man with flowing hair. The man was wearing a buckskin suit and a coonskin cap. Now he was standing up boldly, calmly reloading his rifle. More than a hundred Mexican infantrymen returned his fire but their shots fell far short of the wall and the tall man made no effort to duck.

"Who is that man?" Lopez asked.

"I don't know, Colonel," the sergeant answered. "I know only that he never misses. Never has there been a marksman like that one."

Lopez looked back toward the body of the colonel. Now, Soldana's command would fall to Lopez and he would have the honor of leading the assault against the Texans' fort. "Bury him," he said, pointing to the fallen colonel.

"Should we not report his death to General Santa Anna?" one of the staff officers asked.

"The general has more important things to consider than the fact that one of his commanders was so foolish as to get himself killed by a sharpshooter. I will tell the general that Soldana is dead when I think the time is right. Obey my orders and bury him."

"Yes, Colonel," the staff officer replied and half a dozen men leaped to respond to Lopez's orders.

Chapter 16

L uke surveyed the scene before him. In the distance, he could see the Alamo, a great bastion spread out over several acres of ground. Flags waved from all four corners of the fort and he could see the defenders moving along the top of the walls.

Surrounding the Alamo was the largest assembly of troops Luke had ever seen. Tents, wagons, horses, cannon, and brightly uniformed soldiers were everywhere. Bursts of smoke drifted across the field, followed by a distant thunder. The sound, he knew, was the firing of the cannon and, from his position, he could see the black balls flying swiftly toward the fort. Some disappeared over the walls to land inside but many hit the walls, sending showers of splinters from their impact.

Luke tried to figure out a way to get inside the Alamo. No matter which way he went, he would have to pass through the Mexican Army, and he would have to cover more than three hundred yards of open territory.

Finally, he decided that the only way to get inside was simply to saunter in. Surely the Mexicans wouldn't be looking for anyone trying to get into the Alamo—just out of it. With a bit of luck, he would be halfway there before they realized what he was up to.

Luke took a deep breath, then slapped his heels against his horse's sides. He clucked at the stallion and leaned far forward as he urged him forward.

The horse broke out of the thicket at full gallop. Unfortunately for Luke, a nearby defilade concealed an entire company of Mexican troops and he suddenly found himself in their midst. At that, he might have made it through had not one quick-thinking Mexican soldier waved a blanket in front of Luke's horse. Traveler, already nervous from the cannonade, reared wildly, unseating Luke. A dozen soldiers were on him in an instant.

"So, Colonel Calhoun, we meet again," Lopez said when Luke was brought to him. Lopez smiled broadly at his good luck.

"Isn't this a little out of your line, Lopez?" Luke spat. "These are real soldiers, preparing for a real battle. I thought you fought only women."

Lopez chuckled. "I must confess that there was a time when I was in dishonor among my countrymen," he said. "But after this victory, my honor and the honor of my country will be redeemed."

"There will be no honor in this victory, believe me," Luke said. "All of America is watching what is going on here. You can't win. Even if you kill everyone inside, you can't win."

"We shall see about that," Lopez said. "You see, we

intend to do just that—kill everyone inside the Alamo."

"Women and children as well?"

"If there are women and children inside, the responsibility for their death will lie with the defenders, for they had the opportunity to abandon the fort before we arrived."

"They couldn't do that," Luke said. "They are honorable men. But of course, you know nothing about honor."

"Tell me, Colonel Calhoun," Lopez said, ignoring Luke's insult, "why were you trying to reach the Alamo? Are you eager to die?"

Luke looked down at the ground for a moment. "There is someone in there I want to kill."

"What? You were going into a doomed fort where everyone is going to die anyway, and where you would have died, in order to kill someone?"

"You don't understand," Luke said. "I said I want to kill him."

"Why?"

Luke told Lopez how Joiner had murdered his wife and how, more recently, he had raped his young niece and then allowed his men to use her.

"Yes," Lopez said when the story was completed, "such a man deserves to die." He rubbed his chin and looked at Luke. "I have no choice, you know," he went on. "You will have to be killed."

"Yes, I know," Luke said.

"However, despite what you believe, I am a man of honor," Lopez said. "I will demonstrate that honor by allowing you to live until after the Alamo has fallen.

Before you die, you will be able to see with your own eyes the body of the man you have described."

"There is one more favor I would ask of you," Luke said.

"*Señor*, you are in no position to ask for favors," Lopez informed him.

"This I know," Luke said. "But I will ask anyway, in hopes that you will consider it."

"What favor do you ask?"

"Caroline Lafont, the woman you once kidnapped, is inside the Alamo."

Lopez's eyes opened wide at the news and Luke thought he saw them flash with some inner light. For a moment, he wished he had not mentioned Caroline's name.

"Let her live," Luke said. "Give her a horse and let her ride away."

"Why is she there? I thought she was looking for her father."

"Her father is there," Luke said.

Lopez looked shocked at first—then he laughed. "She has willingly come to a place to die?"

"Yes, and I beg you to let her live," Luke said.

Lopez stroked his chin and looked toward the Alamo.

Again, a distant light flared in his eyes. "I suppose that could be arranged," he said. "With the proper cooperation."

"I'll cooperate," Luke said quickly. "I'll do whatever you ask."

"It isn't your cooperation I'm concerned with," Lopez said with a smile. "It's the girl's."

Luke looked away quickly, the bile rising in his

throat and his face flaming in anger. Better to have said nothing than to subject Caroline to Lopez's evil demands.

———

INSIDE THE ALAMO, the defenders worked hard, shoring up fortifications that had been damaged by the cannonade, repositioning guns that the cannonballs had knocked from their mounts. The men dug trenches within the plaza itself in the event the walls were breached and they positioned ammunition, water, and food at various places in case they were besieged within the fort.

Jim Bowie's illness had almost overtaken him but he remained active in the defense preparations. He had his men carry his cot from one part of the fort to another in order to allow him to give instructions and encouragement.

Colonel Travis had one last ace to play. There was under his command a Mexican named Juan Seguin who had chosen to fight on the side of the Texans.

The Mexicans had made several unsuccessful assaults on the fort, over the last few days, and had been turned back each time, often after losing several men. On one such foray, a Mexican officer was killed close enough to the fort to allow the Texans to recover his body and Juan Seguin was given his uniform to wear. It was Travis's intention to let Seguin slip out during the night, carrying one last desperate appeal for help. Because he was Mexican and because he wore a Mexican uniform, Seguin had a good chance of getting through.

Travis authorized the married men to write one last letter to their wives. A man named Isaac Millsaps approached Caroline and asked her to write a letter for him. She couldn't turn down his request, though she dreaded the task of writing what might very well be his last words to his wife. Nevertheless, she located pen and paper and wrote the letter Millsaps dictated.

My dear dear ones,

We are in the fortress of the Alamo, a ruined church that has almost fell down. The Mexicans are here in large numbers. They have kept up a constant fire since they got here. All of our boys are well and Captain Martin is in good spirits. Early this morning, I watched the Mexicans drilling just out of range. They was marching up and down with such order. They have bright red and blue uniforms and many cannons. Some here at this place believe that the main army has not come up yet. I think they is all here, even Santa Anna. Colonel Bowie is down sick and had to be to bed. I saw him yesterday and he is still ready to fight. He didn't know me from last spring but he did remember Washington. He tells all that help will be here soon and it makes us feel good. We have beef and corn to eat but no coffee. The bag I had fell off on the way here so it was all spilt. I have not seen Travis but two times since he told us that Fannin was going to be here with many men and there would be a good fight. He stays on the wall some but mostly to his room. I hope help comes soon 'cause we can't fight them all. Some says he is going to talk some tonight and group us better for defense. If we fail here, get to the river with the children. All Texas will be before the enemy. We get so little news, we know nothing. There is no discontent in our boys. Some are tired

from lack of sleep and rest. The Mexicans are shooting
every four minutes but most of the shots fall inside and do
no harm. I don't know what else to say. They is calling for
all letters. Kiss the dear children for me and believe as I do
that all will be well and God protects us all.

Isaac.

IF ANY MEN come through there tell them to hurry with
the powder for it is short. I hope you get this and know I
love you all.

Colonel Seguin carried the letters out that night
with Godspeed from everyone in the fort. There was
very little sleeping that night because the Mexican
cannon kept up its firing all night long. Most of the
men of the Alamo remained at their posts, while the
women moved to the sacristy.

Caroline helped Susanna put Angelina to bed.
Then the two women sat on the floor with their backs
to the wall and talked.

It was dark in the room. They dared not light a
candle lest the light attract the Mexican artillery fire.
Occasionally, one of the Texas guns would answer the
Mexican fire and, when a gun inside the fort fired, it
would send out a flash of light a little like lightning,
followed immediately by its own thunder. That flash
of light was the only illumination in the room.

"Susanna, why are you in here?" Caroline asked.
"Why didn't you leave when you had the
opportunity?"

"I don't know, really," Susanna answered. "I guess
Almeron and I never thought it would come down to
this. Besides, where would I go? San Antonio is our

home. Almeron has a good business as a blacksmith there."

"But to put yourself inside a fort during a siege—" Caroline said.

Susanna laughed and, though Caroline couldn't see it, she could imagine the pretty young woman pushing her blond hair back from her face as was her habit.

"Listen to you!" Susanna said. "When I came in here, I didn't know we would undergo a siege. You came in after the siege had already started."

"Yes," Caroline said. "I guess you're right."

"We both are in here for the same reason, I suppose," Susanna said. "We are here because there is someone here that we love."

"Yes," Caroline said. "I came here for the love of one man and I am staying for the love of another."

"Your father and who is the other?"

"I am speaking about Luke Calhoun."

"Oh, do you know Mr. Calhoun?"

"Yes," Caroline said. Then, more quietly she added, "That is, I knew him. He was killed."

"I'm sorry to hear that," Susanna said. "Though I must confess that the thought of death does not seem as final as it once did. Tell me about Luke Calhoun. Did you love him?"

"Yes," Caroline said. There in the darkness of the room, with the sound of the guns outside, Caroline told her story. She spoke of Frank Sweeny and how she had left Louisiana to find her father and save their home. She told of meeting Luke Calhoun and she spoke of Gonzara and Lopez and of the fight in the saloon in which Luke was wounded. Then she told of deceiving Luke by leaving for the Alamo while he lay wounded.

"He cannot have thought well of me as he died," Caroline said. "That is my great regret."

Susanna reached over and squeezed Caroline's hand. "If the soul survives, then we must believe that Luke Calhoun sees you now and understands why you acted as you did."

"Do you believe the soul survives?" Caroline asked.

"Yes, of course. Don't you?"

"I—I suppose so," Caroline said. "But it was easy to say in the past. I've never had to come face to face with death before now."

"Now is when the truth of it is most evident to me," Susanna said.

The two women talked a little longer but, after a while, they grew quiet and, despite the cannonade, managed to drift off to sleep.

Chapter 17

The next morning, Friday, March 4, 1836, the defenders of the Alamo saw that, during the night, the Mexicans had moved their cannon to within two hundred fifty yards of the Alamo. Now, the guns were so close that when they fired against the walls, the stone chips flew like hail across the plaza.

The Mexicans kept up their firing all day long. Caroline and the other women carried water to the Texans at their station but they had to be alert to dodge the shells.

Ben was at the artillery command post at the south end of the west wall. He smiled as Caroline handed him a dipperful of water and he reached out and put his hand on her hair.

"Caroline," he said, "how I wish I had never met you."

"Why, Ben Nichols, how can you say such a thing? Don't you like me?" she teased.

"I'm sorry I got you mixed up in this. I will go to meet my Maker knowing that it is my fault you are here in the Alamo when you could be somewhere else, safe."

"That simply isn't true and you know it," Caroline said. "I was going to come here by myself. If you hadn't come along to help me, I might have been killed out on the trail. Then I would never have seen my father again."

"You've not had much time to enjoy the reunion, have you?"

Caroline smiled at Ben. "I've enjoyed the time I *have* had."

"Miss Lafont?" someone farther down the line called. "Could I have some water, please?"

Ben let his hand drop from her. "Go," he said. "Tend to the others. I don't think we have much time left. Those cannons can't get any closer without the Mexicans staging an all-out attack."

Caroline moved along the parapet to give water to the others.

"Say, Miss Lafont, I would have a word with you," someone said, as Caroline climbed down the ladder from the parapet where she had been working.

The man who spoke was the evil-looking one with the cross-shaped scar on his cheek. He rubbed the scar and narrowed his green eyes as he looked at her. Despite the danger of the situation, Caroline felt uneasy around him.

"Do you want some water?" she offered, holding up the dipper.

"I don't want no water," the man said. "Colonel Travis tells me you got near a hunnert 'n fifty dollars' worth of gold."

"Yes," Caroline said, "I do." *What difference did it*

make? she thought. The gold was worthless if they were all going to die.

"Well, I was sent here by Sam Houston to get that gold."

"That's a lie," Caroline said boldly. "General Houston didn't know I had the gold and, even if he did, he wouldn't have sent for it."

"He didn't know 'bout *your* gold," Joiner said, "but he figured there was *some* gold here, so he sent me to collect up what I could and take it back to him. It's for the glory of Texas, you unnerstan', and also to keep the gold from fallin' into the hands o' the Mexicans."

"I have news for you and for General Sam Houston," Caroline said, furious now. "I'm going to give my life for the glory of Texas and that is quite enough, thank you. I have no intention of giving up my gold."

In truth, Caroline had been so moved by the courage and determination of the Texans that she would have gladly given up her gold if she could have been certain it would go where it would do some good. But she knew, instinctively, that Joiner would keep the gold for himself.

Joiner rubbed his scar and looked at her with his narrow, piercing eyes. "I'll have to come up with some way to change your mind," he said menacingly.

"Caroline?" Susanna called. "Won't you help me with the next meal?"

Glad that Susanna's summons had taken her away from this man, Caroline hurried toward the cooking fire, with only a glance over her shoulder toward Joiner.

"Do you know that man?" her friend asked.

"No," Caroline said. "I never saw him before he came here."

"I have never met a man who filled me with such feeling of uneasiness," Susanna said. "He gives me the shudders."

"I know what you mean," Caroline said.

"Almeron believes the attack will come tomorrow."

"Oh, Sue," Caroline said. "Do you really think it will come tomorrow?"

"Yes," Susanna said. "Yes, I do."

Caroline blinked several times and tears began to roll down her cheeks. She was glad she had talked with her father that morning and told him she loved him.

"We've all known it was coming," Susanna said soothingly. She put her arms around Caroline.

"Yes, I know," Caroline said. She smiled. "I'm sorry. Please forgive me."

"There is nothing to forgive. I guess I've cried so much I have no tears left."

"Susanna, I have never met a braver woman than you."

"Oh, I don't know about that," Susanna said. "You are facing the same dangers just as bravely."

"Yes," Caroline teased with a broad smile. "We are both brave, aren't we?"

"Oh, Caroline, I have a wonderful idea," Susanna said, clapping her hands like the young girl she was. "Let's us have supper together tonight. You and your father, Almeron and me and Angelina. Oh, it'll be ever so nice, just as if the two of you had come to our house in normal times."

"Yes," Caroline said and, though she tried to stop

them, the tears began to flow again. This time, the tears were for the sense of loss she felt at having lost Luke without him knowing that she cared and knowing that her long trip was all for naught as she and her father would soon die.

Caroline and Susanna took the noon meal around to the men on their posts, dodging the shot and shell that continued to rain down on the plaza. After the meal was served to everyone, the two women planned their evening. They gathered what tableware they could find in the mission and found a cloth that would be suitable for a tablecloth.

"I have two dresses," Susanna said as they put the last touches on the table. "You may have first choice."

"I couldn't do that," Caroline said. "They are yours."

"I won't enjoy putting on a fresh dress unless you do as well."

"Very well, but you must have first choice," Caroline insisted.

"Let's pick them out now," Susanna suggested.

One of the dresses was red with ruffles, the other a plain blue. Susanna spread them out on the bed in the room she had shared with Almeron until the shelling had started in earnest. She stood there with her finger on her chin, looking at them.

"Oh, Caroline, you wear the blue dress. It will really bring out the color of your eyes."

Caroline picked up the dress and held it to her. She closed her eyes and recalled the last time she had dressed for a party. It was in New Orleans and it seemed like a lifetime ago.

"I have known you but such a short time but I have

never had a better friend in my life than you," Caroline said and she put her arms around Susanna and embraced her.

"We are going to have such a fine time tonight that Santa Anna can just go to blazes," Susanna said and she and Caroline laughed.

The afternoon passed quickly as Susanna and Caroline prepared a special supper. Before supper, however, Travis called another meeting of his men and Henri and Almeron had to attend. The two women stood under the sally port and listened as Travis spoke in a quiet but determined tone. Then he unsheathed his sword and drew a line in the dirt.

"Gentlemen, it is clear to me now that we can expect no aid," he said. "All who remain here with me can have only one hope and that is to realize a valiant death. With that as my only promise, I ask those of you who wish to stand by me to cross this line."

With a hurrah, every man but one crossed the line. The one who remained behind was Louis Rose, a veteran of the Napoleonic Wars. No one looked toward him.

Later, as Caroline and her father shared their supper with Susanna and Almeron, the gaiety of their conversation belied the situation. The gaiety may have been forced, but it was there nonetheless.

Angelina cried for attention once and her mother picked her up and played with her. The little girl laughed and Caroline reached over to touch her.

"That is what I regret most," Caroline said. "I will never have a child."

Susanna handed the baby over to Caroline. "We will share this precious little girl," she said.

Caroline held the baby close to her and felt the tiny fingers plucking at her.

"It's getting late," Susanna said a few moments later.

"It's not late," Almeron said, puzzled by his wife's statement.

"Yes, it is," Susanna said pointedly. Suddenly, Almeron realized what she was saying and he smiled.

"Oh," he said. "Yes, it is getting late."

Chapter 18

"Where is Colonel Soldana?" Santa Anna asked. He had called a meeting of all his commanders and Lopez had responded as commander of the First Fusiliers.

"He is dead, General," Lopez said casually.

"How can he be dead?" Santa Anna asked. "The First Fusiliers have not made an assault against the walls yet. I have purposely held them back."

"He was killed by the tall Texan in buckskin," Lopez said.

"The one called Crockett," another officer put in.

"David Crockett, General," Lopez explained. "He is famous in America. He was once a member of Congress, I believe."

"And I am the ruler of all of Mexico," Santa Anna said. "I consider it an affront for a lowly member of the American Congress to challenge me. Why does he take such risks?"

"General," a young officer explained, "Crockett has already killed more than a score of our men from over three hundred yards away. He is a devil with the long gun, that one."

"Well, we shall see how effective his one gun is against my entire army. Gentlemen, tomorrow morning, before dawn, we will attack. Here is a map of the citadel, prepared by one of my engineers."

Santa Anna spread the map out on a small field table and all of his commanders gathered around.

"I shall divide my infantrymen into four columns, each of which shall contain eight hundred men. Two columns will attack the north wall, one from the east and the other from the west. A third column will attack the east wall, and the fourth column, led by you, Colonel Lopez, will attack the palisade from the south, here, nearest the church."

"That is the place where David Crockett stands," Lopez said, smiling. "It will be my pleasure to attack there."

"I will direct the attack from here." Santa Anna pointed to a spot about five hundred yards from the wall. "I will keep four hundred men in reserve."

The cavalry commander said, "You have given no position for the cavalry, Excellency."

"The cavalry will be held at the ready," Santa Anna said. "If the Texans try to break out, you will run them down." He took a deep breath. "And you will kill them," he added.

"When will the attack begin?" Lopez asked.

"We will move into position at one o'clock in the morning," Santa Anna said. "We will crawl forward silently on our bellies and, at the break of dawn, we will strike."

"That's a very good plan, General," several of the

officers said and Santa Anna smiled and nodded in response to their servile compliments.

"I have conceived the master plan," Santa Anna said. "Now I call on you, Colonel Lopez, to work out the details."

"But, General," Lopez protested, "I have just learned of the attack."

"The attack is carefully planned. It is the other things, the details of supply and movement, which I ask you to arrange. If you are not capable, tell me and I will find someone who is competent."

Lopez cleared his throat. "General, I will do as you ask."

Lopez studied the map as the other commanders stared at him. He knew that they were secretly enjoying his discomfort, and he knew also that they were glad Santa Anna hadn't put them on the spot.

"Issue each musket bearer ten rounds of ammunition," Lopez said. "And give every fiftieth man a scaling ladder and some picks and spikes."

"Very good, Colonel," Santa Anna said. The other commanders brooded over the fact that Lopez had successfully risen to the challenge thrown him by Santa Anna.

"See that the men are fed and let them get as much rest as possible between now and the time we attack," Lopez went on. "And end the cannonade."

"Why?" Santa Anna said.

"General, for eleven days we have been shelling the Texans. It has done nothing except unnerve them. If we end it suddenly, they will be even more unnerved."

Santa Anna smiled. "Perhaps you are right. Very well, I will stop the barrage."

"General, we are flying the red flag. You have demanded unconditional surrender. If they refuse, you will put the entire garrison to the sword. Am I correct?"

"Yes. These perfidious foreigners must be taught a lesson," Santa Anna said.

"Very well. Instruct the buglers to play *Degüello*."

"*Fire and Death*," Santa Anna said, smiling.

"Have them play in relays, so that the bugle calls can be heard by the Texans throughout the night."

"Yes," Santa Anna said, smiling broadly and slapping his hand against his thigh. "Yes, Don Esteban, that is a marvelous idea."

Lopez had suddenly moved up to a first-name basis with his cousin and the other commanders now realized that Lopez was the most influential of them all. Their contempt for him suddenly turned to servile respect.

Lopez returned to his own command, then sent word by couriers to all the subordinate commanders within his area of responsibility. The word traveled fast and the firing soon ceased as the men lay down to get what rest they could. By nightfall, an uneasy quiet had descended over the land.

The bugler began the *Degüello* and the plaintive notes drifted out loud and clear—then returned in a haunting echo from the walls of the Alamo.

Lopez paced about nervously, then rode among his commanders to make certain all was in readiness.

Luke called out to Lopez as he returned just after

midnight from his final inspection ride. Luke was tied to the wheel of a wagon.

Lopez smiled at him. "You must be wondering what is happening," Lopez said. He pointed toward the looming shadow of the Alamo in the distance. "Tomorrow, our flag will fly from inside the Alamo. The bugle call you hear means we will give no quarter, take no prisoners."

"You intend to murder them all?" Luke asked.

"Murder, Colonel? But this is war. One does not murder in war. One is either the victor or the vanquished. I do not intend to be the vanquished."

Luke pulled at the ropes that restrained him but he couldn't get loose.

"Free me," Luke said. "Let me go to the Alamo to die with brave men."

"I have other plans for you." Lopez laughed and walked away from the distraught Luke Calhoun.

Lopez and his officers began waking the troops who had managed to go to sleep. Armed with muskets and ten rounds of ammunition apiece, the men began moving forward quietly.

The moon and stars were hidden by clouds and the night was cold. The men shivered convulsively, though perhaps as much from fear as from the chill night air.

By four o'clock, nearly every man was in position, lying on the cold ground, quietly waiting. Near the position Lopez had taken, an owl hooted. In the distance, a coyote howled.

The cry of the coyote awakened Caroline.

When Caroline stepped outside, she saw her father looking out over the plaza. Beyond him stood the final defensive line erected by the engineers. A circular palisade, made of dirt and cowhide, formed a small fortress outside each room. If the walls were breached, the defenders would fall back to the low barracks and fight from inside the rooms. The thought of a battle occurring here, in this very room, frightened Caroline.

Henri turned to see his daughter standing there.

"Listen," he said.

"I don't hear anything except the bugler," she replied.

"That's just it," Henri said. "The bombardment has stopped. That can only mean the Mexicans are about to attack."

"Oh," Caroline said anxiously. "Do you really think so?"

"Yes, I am sure of it. Now, here's what I want you to do," he said. "Go to the sacristy and stay there. Don't come out for any reason until the shooting has completely stopped. There is a possibility that the Mexicans will spare the women and the children."

Caroline shuddered.

"Tell me you'll do what I say," Henri said. "I'll feel much easier if I know you have a chance."

"I'll do it," Caroline promised.

Henri embraced his daughter for what Caroline knew would be the very last time, then he walked away into the chill night air.

———

IN THE EAST, a faint streak of pink began to lighten the sky. Soon, it would be dawn and the attack would begin. Lopez felt an uneasiness in the pit of his stomach and he knew that if he held his hand before his eyes, he would be able to detect a quiver. He was growing anxious for the attack to begin. Once it was underway, he would be all right, he knew.

The anxiety Lopez felt also plagued his troops. They were beginning to fidget and whisper among themselves. Finally, one of the soldiers could keep silent no longer. He rose to his feet and shouted at the top of his voice, *"Viva Santa Anna!"*

"Viva Santa Anna!" a hundred voices echoed. Then the shout was taken up by thousands and the lone bugler was joined by a score of others, all sounding the attack. The troops surged forward and the darkness of the morning was filled with the rolling thunder of thousands of running feet as the Mexican soldiers rushed toward the Alamo.

"Viva Santa Anna!"

———

THERE WAS ONLY a tiny amount of coffee left, and the defenders of the Alamo had saved it for this very hour. Ben, Almeron, and Captain John Baugh stood on the wall nursing their coffee and wondering when the attack would begin. When they heard the shouts and the bugles and the rumble of running feet, they knew that this was the moment.

"Say a prayer, boys," Ben said quietly. "This is it!"

"I'll inform Colonel Travis," Captain Baugh said. He scrambled down the ladder and ran across the plaza to the room where Travis lay sleeping.

"Colonel Travis!" he called. "The Mexicans are coming!"

William Barret Travis leaped up from his bed.

"Joe," Travis called.

"Yes, sir?"

"I want you to go to the sacristy and look out for the women and the child."

"I'd rather fight with you, sir."

"Joe, believe me, it would give me more peace of mind to know that you were looking out for them."

"Yes, sir, I'll go."

Travis grabbed his sword and shotgun and raced across the plaza toward the ladder on the north wall.

"Here they come, Colonel," Ben said as Travis and Baugh joined him.

Out of the morning darkness came the shadowy figures of hundreds and hundreds of Mexican soldiers. They were all shouting now. Some were issuing challenges—others were just shouting to keep up their own courage.

"We're loaded and ready, Colonel," one of the artillerymen said to Travis.

"As soon as you have them within range, blast away!" Travis said. "Then reload and fire again as quickly as you can!"

"They're in range, Colonel!" one of the riflemen shouted.

"Open fire!" Travis replied.

The Texas riflemen opened fire from their position on top of the walls and the cannon raked the charging mass of Mexicans with the cut bits of horseshoe that Almeron had prepared for them. The Mexican attackers fell in waves.

"Hurrah, m'boys! Hurrah!" Travis shouted.

The Texans were cool and collected and they took

careful aim before firing. Every volley felled as many Mexicans as there were shots fired. Many of the Texans had three or four rifles loaded and at the ready. As soon as they fired one, they picked up another and aimed at a new target.

The column of Mexicans attacking the north wall stopped advancing. The men began to mill around, dazed and disoriented by the murderous fire that the Texans poured down on them.

Colonel Travis walked up and down the wall, shouting encouragement to his troops. He fired both barrels of his shotgun down into the mass of Mexican soldiers below him. "Well, Ben, how do you think they liked that?" he asked with a smile.

As Ben turned to answer him, he heard an angry buzzing sound. Then, to his horror, a hole appeared in the middle of Travis's forehead. Blood spurted, and Travis's eyes rolled upward as he dropped the shotgun over the edge of the wall and staggered backward.

Ben reached for him but Travis tumbled over the edge of the parapet and fell heavily to the ground below. Ben ran to the edge and looked down. Amazingly, Travis was sitting up. He turned his head from side to side as if trying to figure out where he was.

"Colonel, sit still. Someone will help you!" Ben shouted down at him but, even as he called out, Travis fell back and his head rolled to one side. His eyes remained open but unseeing. Colonel Travis was dead.

"Travis?" Almeron asked as Ben returned to his position.

"He's dead," Ben said.

"He's one of the lucky ones. He went early."

Almeron raised his rifle to his shoulder and fired again.

Ben could see the Mexican officers running behind their men, urging them forward by hitting them with the flat surfaces of their saber blades. The Mexican soldiers came forward again and again, only to be beaten back by deadly accurate rifle fire and murderous grapeshot.

———

IN THE SACRISTY, Caroline, Suzanna, Angelina, three Mexican women, and four Mexican children huddled together. Joe was standing in the doorway looking out.

Joiner came into the sacristy then. "Get out of the way," he said, pushing Joe to one side.

"Colonel Joiner, what are you doing in here?" Caroline asked. "Why aren't you out with Colonel Travis and the others?"

"Travis is dead," Joiner said bluntly. "I'm in charge now."

"Wouldn't that be Colonel Bowie?" Caroline asked.

"Nah, that sick son of a bitch can't do nothin'," Joiner said. He held out his hand. "I'll take that hunnert 'n fifty dollars you're holdin'."

"What? I offered it to Colonel Travis and he said it couldn't do any good now."

"Yeah, well, he was probably talkin' about usin' the money for Texas. I plan to keep the money for myself, so hand it over." Joiner held out his left hand, palm up.

"No," Caroline said, drawing back from him.

Joiner raised his pistol and pointed it at her.

"You're probably goin' to die anyway but I don't have time to wait, 'cause I don't plan to be around when Mexicans get in. So I reckon I'll just kill you now and..."

Joiner's declaration was interrupted by the sound of a gunshot. Joiner went down with a bullet hole in his temple and when Caroline looked over toward Joe, she saw that he was holding a smoking pistol in his hand.

"Oh, Joe, thank you, thank you!" Caroline said.

"Yes'm. Colonel Travis told me to look out for the women folk 'n, even if he's dead now, I still plan to do what he told me to do."

On the third wave, the column that was striking the northwest corner began to drift east. The eastern column, which had been beaten back by the defenders, moved to the north, and both columns merged with the northeast column. Now, all three columns formed one solid mass of men, and that mass surged toward the walls of the Alamo, only to have the front ranks cut down like grass before a scythe.

The Mexicans' scaling ladders, spikes, and picks were all gone now, dropped and trampled to useless sticks under the mad rush. The column reached the fort but, without ladders, they had no way to scale the walls. They milled around in frustration for a quarter of an hour while the Texas riflemen poured down murderous fire from close range.

Lopez was attacking the south wall and, because most of the Texans had rallied to the larger attack, he was meeting with less resistance. He rushed ahead of his men and began to scale the wall. His soldiers, inspired by his courage, climbed the wall behind him.

Lopez seemed to lead a charmed life. Bullets were whizzing all around him and, to each side of him, his men were dropping, mortally wounded, but he remained unscathed.

Behind him, a military band had taken up the *Degüello*, and Lopez realized that Santa Anna had committed his final reserves to the battle. The fresh troops began firing so excitedly that their bullets hit Lopez's men. He was sustaining as much damage from his own troops as he was from the Texas defenders.

"Inside," Lopez shouted. "We must get inside!"

He managed to tumble over the top of the wall and several of his men followed him. The Mexicans were now inside the Alamo!

Lopez ran down to the gate and opened it. Then the Mexicans came pouring through in a solid stream, shouting challenges at the Texans, who answered with their own calls of defiance.

The Mexicans and the Texans met in the plaza. They fired only one round from their rifles before resorting to pistols, and finally to knives, bayonets, swords, clubs, and even their bare hands.

In command now, Captain Baugh shouted for the Texans to withdraw to their final defensive line, the semicircle of parapets built around the doors of the rooms in the low barracks.

Ben looked toward the plaza and saw Henri Lafont lying dead. He hadn't seen him fall and he hoped Henri had had a quick, clean death. He closed his eyes against the sight of his friend's corpse and then turned to look toward the church, hoping that the women and children inside were safe. The church had not come under direct attack, though it had been struck by several cannonballs. Davy Crockett and his Tennesseans were close to the church, trying to fight their way to the low barracks to join in the final defensive battle.

The Mexicans had poured into the Alamo in numbers that gave them almost a twenty-to-one superiority over the Texans. They surrounded Davy Crockett and the six men who remained with him. The Tennesseans fought hard, loading and firing, then stabbing with their knives and bayonets as the enemy soldiers rushed them.

Many of the Mexicans recognized Davy Crockett as the "devil with the long gun" who had shot so many of them over the last few days and they were anxious to avenge the deaths of their comrades. They took careful aim and fired, but not one of their bullets found its mark. Then Ben saw a Mexican lieutenant lunge up behind Crockett and slash him just above the eye with a ferocious blow from his sword. Davy Crockett fell to the ground and, within moments, more than twenty Mexicans had attacked him with bayonets.

Ben looked again toward the church. As he turned, he felt a blow to the back of his neck and he pitched forward. A second later, there was an explosion inside his head as a bullet crashed into his brain.

Caroline crept through the church to peer through a crack in the door. She turned her head away from the sight of her father lying dead in the plaza. When she looked back, she saw a cannonball blow away another parapet—then she realized that the Mexicans had captured all the defenders' cannons and had turned them on the low barracks. They blew away all the parapets one by one.

Caroline heard a shout and saw several Mexican soldiers carrying the body of Jim Bowie impaled on their bayonets. The soldiers' faces and clothing had turned red from his dripping blood.

One of the Texas artillerymen suddenly appeared in the plaza near the church. His face was blackened with powder from the gun blasts and his eyes were wide in shock and horror.

"Miss, you'd best get back away from the door," he shouted. He'd barely got his warning out when he was felled by a bullet.

"Come back, Miss Caroline, please," Joe called.

Caroline ran back to the sacristy. She saw Robert Evans, the man who had been carrying powder from the magazine to the defenders. He had been grievously wounded and was crawling toward the powder magazine, carrying a torch. He managed to make it to the powder room and, a moment later, Caroline heard a tremendously loud explosion.

"Listen ..." Caroline finally said and the others realized that it was deathly quiet. After an hour and a half of deafening explosions, there was now only silence. The battle was over.

Chapter 19

The sun was well up now and the sky was light. It was six-thirty in the morning, just an hour and a half after Ben Nichols had first sounded the alarm. Moments before, there had been the explosion of cannons and the crash of balls against the barricades, punctuated by the sharper sound of musketry and the screams of dying and wounded men. Now an eerie silence had descended on the fort. Susanna and Caroline stood together, their hearts in their throats. They knew what the silence meant for their men and they were preparing themselves for what was to happen to them.

The door to the sacristy opened and a Mexican officer stepped inside. Smoke drifted in through the open door wreathing his face in a ghostlike haze as his piercing black eyes surveyed the room.

"Mrs. Dickinson?" he asked.

Caroline felt Susanna tremble and she squeezed her hand.

"If you value your life, woman, speak up!" the Mexican officer said sharply. As he stepped forward, Caroline could see blood on his tunic. Was it his blood or the blood of an American he had killed? Was it her father's blood?

Susanna took a deep breath and stepped forward, carrying Angelina.

"I am Mrs. Dickinson," she said. She closed her eyes and prepared herself for whatever fate awaited her. Two Mexican soldiers started to seize her but the officer who had summoned her spoke sharply to them, and they stepped back.

"What are you going to do with her?" Caroline demanded.

The officer looked at her. "Are you the one called Caroline?" he asked.

Speechless with fear, Caroline nodded.

"There is an old friend of yours outside," the officer said. "He is eager to see you. Come with me, please," he ordered.

The two women followed the officer outside. Hundreds and hundreds of Mexican bodies lay in the plaza. When Caroline saw one dead Texan surrounded by many Mexicans, she realized how fiercely the Texans had fought.

She saw Davy Crockett's body lying between the church and the barracks, his cap by his side.

Suddenly a shot rang out. Susanna screamed and fell, bleeding profusely, still cradling her baby daughter in her arms.

"Who fired that shot?" the officer demanded angrily. No one answered. "The next man to fire a shot will be summarily executed!" the officer promised. "These ladies are under the protection of the Mexican Army."

A Mexican surgeon was summoned quickly and he began to dress the wound in Susanna's leg.

Caroline was bending over her friend when someone spoke to her.

"So, Caroline, we meet again."

Caroline looked up to see Don Esteban Juan Lopez.

"You?" she said.

"Yes," Lopez said. "As you can see, I have had my honor restored."

"Do you call this honor?"

"It was an honorable battle, well fought," Lopez said.

"It was an expensive battle for you. A thousand or more Mexicans died in this siege."

"One thousand five hundred of our men were killed," Lopez said, shrugging easily. "But it is of no consequence. The significant thing is that we have taught a valuable lesson to those who would make a revolution. We have shown them that they cannot win."

"Is that what this battle was?" Caroline asked. "A lesson?"

"Yes," Lopez said. "And that is the message I want you and Mrs. Dickinson to take to the rest of the world."

"Why should we?" Caroline asked.

"Consider it as payment for your life," another officer said. He was a tall, handsome, impressive-looking man.

"Allow me to present His Excellency, General Santa Anna," Lopez said.

Suddenly, there were several shouts and a babble of voices. Caroline looked toward the sound and saw the Mexicans dragging three Texans to the center of the plaza.

"Not all of your countrymen were heroes, it would appear," Lopez said. "We have found three cowards."

"Four cowards, sir," Joe said, pointing to Joiner's body.

"Who are you?"

"My name is Joe, sir. I'm Colonel Travis' man."

"How is it you weren't killed?"

"Colonel Travis assigned him to look after the women," Caroline said. "And, as you can see, he did his job when that man attempted to murder me." She made no mention of the gold coins.

The three men were the ones who had come with Joiner in search of gold.

"They were hiding, General," an officer reported. "They did not take part in the battle."

"Take the women back into the church," Santa Anna said. "Make certain Mrs. Dickinson's wound is well cared for."

————

Luke Calhoun had been able to follow the course of the battle by listening to the sounds. When it grew quiet, he knew that the Alamo had fallen and now he could see the Mexican tricolors fluttering in the breeze atop the walls.

It was nearly eight o'clock when Lopez swung

down from his horse and smiled at Luke. "As you can see," he said, "the battle is over and we have won."

"It sounded to me as if the Texans gave a good accounting of themselves," Luke said.

Lopez patted his horse's neck. "Perhaps so, but they are all dead now, so what does it matter?"

"All dead?"

Lopez looked at Luke. "No, not all. We killed no women. Caroline is still alive."

"Thank God," Luke said.

"The men you spoke of earlier—the one you wanted to kill. He had a cross on his face?" Lopez asked.

"Yes," Luke said.

"He died a coward's death," Lopez said. He described how Joiner had attempted to murder one of the women, only to be shot by a black servant to Colonel Travis.

"I'm glad he didn't die with brave men," Luke said.

"Many brave men died today," Lopez said.

"Yes," Luke replied, "brave men from both sides."

Lopez looked at him in surprise. "You would grant that a Mexican can show courage?"

"Yes, of course," Luke said. "Why would you have to ask such a thing?"

"Many Texans believe all Mexicans are evil, just as some Mexicans believe all Texans are evil."

"Colonel Lopez, may I see Caroline?"

Lopez stroked his chin. "I must think about this," he said.

From the church, Caroline could see the Mexican soldiers at work in the plaza, loading the bodies of their dead into wagons and then taking them away. Caroline watched wagon after wagon drive away laden with bodies piled high like firewood.

It was late afternoon before the last Mexican body was removed. After that, the soldiers dragged the Texans to the center of the plaza. They piled dry branches and dead men, layer upon layer until the pile of bodies and firewood reached twelve feet high. Then a Mexican officer tossed a torch onto the pile. A few moments later, a tremendous blaze cracked and danced over the funeral pyre as the bodies of all the dead Texans went up in flames. Caroline closed her eyes tightly to hold back her tears as she mourned the death of her father and the deaths of all the brave defenders of the Alamo.

She saw another, smaller fire, a small distance away and, in it, she recognized the boots of the man named Joiner. The Mexican soldiers had enough respect for the brave defenders of the fort not to commit the bodies of heroes and cowards to the same fire.

After watching the flames burn for a while, she turned and went back inside the church.

"What are they doing now?" Susanna asked. She had been in pain most of the afternoon and now she held her throbbing leg.

"Just some cleaning up," Caroline answered. She didn't want to tell Susanna that all the bodies were being burned.

About an hour later, Lopez came to the door again.

"Do you think Mrs. Dickinson can travel?" he asked Caroline.

"I don't know—" Caroline started but Susanna interrupted her.

"Caroline, I want to leave this place. Even if it kills me, I want to get out of here, away from the smell of death."

Caroline smiled wanly. She could well understand the young woman's determination to leave in spite of her injury. In her place, Caroline would have felt the same way.

"Yes," Caroline said. "She can travel. I'll help her."

"I have decided to send someone with you," Lopez said.

"One of your soldiers?"

"No, a Texan," Lopez said. "Someone we captured before the battle. I shall give him an unconditional release."

"Is it someone you caught trying to flee the Alamo?" Caroline asked. "Because if it is, I would rather travel by myself."

Lopez laughed. "No," he said. "We caught this man trying to get *into* the Alamo. Can you imagine someone trying to get inside after we already had it under siege?"

"Who is it?" Caroline asked.

"It doesn't matter," Susanna said. "If he was trying to come inside to help us, then he is a good man."

"Yes," Caroline said. "I suppose you are right."

Lopez disappeared, then returned a short time later "Here he is," he said.

A man stepped inside the sacristy. "Hello, Caroline," he said quietly.

Caroline gasped and leaned against the wall to

keep from falling over in a faint. "Luke?" she said. "I thought you were dead!"

"A great many good men are dead," he said, "but as you can see, I am not." Luke looked at Susanna. "Are you sure you can travel, ma'am?" he asked.

"Yes," Susanna said, though pain strained her features. "Please, let's leave as quickly as we can."

"All right," Luke said. He walked over to Susanna and picked her up in his arms. Then he indicated the baby with a nod. "Caroline, carry the baby, and let's go."

"The black man will go with you," Lopez said.

"What?"

"Luke, he saved my life, and probably the lives of Susanna and Angelina as well. His name is Joe."

Luke smiled, then extended his hand toward Joe. "It will be good to travel with one of the heroes of the Alamo."

Caroline picked up Angelina, who cooed and smiled and reached up to play with her long hair.

Outside, Lopez had four horses waiting for them. Luke put Susanna on one horse, helped Caroline onto the second, handed up the baby to her, then mounted his own stallion.

"Here is your pistol," Lopez said, handing the weapon to Luke. "You may need it against marauding bandits."

"Like the ones you used to lead?" Caroline said.

Lopez smiled. "Precisely," he answered. "Or like the band led by the late 'Colonel' Joiner."

"Let's go," Caroline said and she, Susanna, Luke, and Joe rode out the south gate. The Mexican soldiers, who were now in possession of the fort, looked at them uninterestedly. They, like Caroline and Susanna, seemed to be in shock after all the killing that had taken place earlier.

As soon as they were outside the Alamo, they urged their horses into a canter the more quickly to leave this place behind them.

————

SUSANNA HAD FRIENDS IN GONZALES, so it was to that settlement that they headed.

They had ridden no more than five or six miles away from San Antonio when Susanna's leg wound opened up and they had to stop. By then, it was quite late so Luke suggested that they make camp for the night. The women, though still too close to the Alamo to be free from all their fears, agreed that it was necessary to stop.

"Are you hungry?" Luke asked.

"No," Caroline said. "The events of the day have taken away any appetite I might have had."

"I'm not hungry either," Susanna said, rocking her baby in her arms. "But I know Angelina must be. She hasn't eaten since last night."

Tears came to her eyes and Caroline realized she was thinking of the dinner they had shared. It was only twenty-four hours ago, yet it seemed like days, weeks, even months. It was, in fact, a lifetime ago, for her father and Almeron were both dead now.

"Here," Luke said, handing a piece of beef jerky to Susanna. "Give this to the baby."

"She can't eat this," Susanna protested.

"Yes, she can, if you chew it up for her," Luke said.

"I learned that trick from the Indians. The Indians learned it from the birds."

Susanna began to chew on the tough meat. After a while, she transferred the chewed-up jerky to the baby's mouth and Angelina ate it hungrily.

"Look at her," Susanna said. "Bless her little heart, she was starving, and yet, she has scarcely cried all day."

"She's too young to understand everything that has happened," Luke said. "But she realizes something has." While Susanna was feeding the baby, Luke took the saddle blankets from the horses. He spread one on the ground, then set the other two aside.

"We'll have to share the same blankets," he said. "We have no extra blankets and it will be too cold, otherwise." The women made no comment. Later, the four of them crawled under the blankets and went to sleep. Angelina slept quietly in her mother's arms.

Caroline awoke a short time later and turned to see Luke staring straight up into the night. She, too, looked up at the stars.

"When I was a little girl," she said, "my father told me that every time someone died, a new star was born in heaven," she said. "Do you think that's true?"

"It could be," Luke replied. "Who is to say?"

"My father is up there tonight," Caroline said. "And so is Almeron. For a while, I thought you were dead."

"I don't know how that rumor was started," Luke said.

"When I saw that you were alive, my heart leapt with joy, despite all that had happened." She reached over and took his hand in hers.

Luke moved toward Caroline and cradled her in his arms, where she fell into fitful sleep.

———

SUSANNA'S LEG was somewhat better the next day and they covered several miles. Early in the afternoon, however, three armed men stopped them. They were Mexicans but they didn't appear to be members of any organized military unit. One of them held a pistol leveled at Luke.

"So," the gunman said, smiling broadly, "we have some stinking rebels here."

The other two Mexicans laughed.

"Where are you going?" the leader asked.

"We are on a mission for General Santa Anna," Luke said.

The Mexican laughed. "You are on a mission for El Presidente, eh? I see. And did he ask you to bring along a black man, two women and a baby?"

"That is the mission, yes."

"That is very unusual, *señor*," the Mexican said. "I tell you what. I will take the two women and finish your mission for you."

The Mexican cocked his pistol and fired. A great puff of smoke issued from the pistol and Caroline saw the ball deflect off the saddle in front of Luke's leg. Miraculously, Luke wasn't hit and, quick as a flash, he had his own pistol in his hand. His gun roared and the Mexican pitched from his saddle.

"Get him," one of the other two shouted. "He cannot reload quickly enough."

"I have more bullets in this gun," Luke warned, swinging his gun toward the other two.

The one who had spoken laughed and pulled his own pistol. He pointed it toward Luke and took slow, deliberate aim.

"No!" Luke said. But, even as he spoke, he saw the Mexican pulling the hammer back and he had no choice. He pulled the trigger, and his gun roared a second time.

Now, the one remaining Mexican realized he was not dealing with an ordinary man with an ordinary pistol and he turned and dug his heels into his horse's sides to urge the animal to run.

Despite all the killing and destruction, despite their own grievous losses, Joe, Susanna and Caroline were able to laugh at the spectacle of the Mexican fleeing for his life before the "devil gun" got him as well.

The laughter, the first since the Alamo, felt good.

"Cap'n, sir, would you mind if I jes sort of went my own way?" Joe asked. "I mean, seein' as Colonel Travis don't own me no more on account of he's dead, I'd like to see if I could . . ."

"Yes, Joe, of course you can," Luke replied. "As far as I'm concerned, you've more than earned your freedom."

"Joe?" Caroline said.

"Yes, ma'am?"

Caroline took five twenty-dollar gold pieces from her vest and handed them to him.

"Oh, Miss Caroline, I couldn't take that."

"Nonsense," Caroline said with an appreciative smile. "Don't you think my life is worth a hundred dollars?"

A wide smile spread across Joe's face as he took the money. "Yes'm it most surely is worth a hunnert dollars."

With a wave of goodbye, Joe went on his own way while Luke, Caroline, Susanna, and Angelina continued on to Gonzales.

Chapter 20

Five days later, the little party reached Gonzales where they were greeted by Major General Sam Houston. Three-inch rowels, shaped like daisies, jingled from Houston's spurs, and a long red feather fluttered over his white hat. Several men helped the women dismount and Houston invited them into the tavern he was using as his temporary headquarters.

"We heard a couple of days ago that the Alamo had fallen," Houston said anxiously. "Is that true?"

"Yes," Luke said. "It is true."

"How many of our men were lost?"

Nearly everyone in Gonzales had gathered around to hear the news. Many were women and Luke could tell by their anxious faces that they had loved ones in the Alamo. "All of our men were lost," he said.

"Prisoners?"

"None," Luke said. "They were all killed."

"No!" one of the women screamed.

"The volunteers from Gonzales, too?" another asked.

"All of them," Luke said. "One hundred and eighty-three men. Only the women and children were spared."

"I don't ask this by way of criticism, you understand," Houston said, "but how is it you were spared?"

"He was captured as he tried to get into the Alamo *before* the battle," Caroline spoke up quickly. "And he was spared so that he could bring you a message from Santa Anna."

"All right," General Houston said. "What is the message you bring from the Napoleon of the West?"

"Santa Anna has vowed to drive all Americans out of Texas, once and forever," Luke said.

"He dared to make such a boast? And how does he intend to back it up?" Houston asked.

"With men and guns," Luke said. "General, he brought five thousand men with him to the Alamo. I am pleased to report, however, that he lost fifteen hundred in the siege."

"Fifteen hundred of Santa Anna's men were killed by one hundred-eighty-three of our own?"

"Yes," Luke said. "I saw scores of wagons departing the Alamo, all of them carrying bodies of Mexican soldiers."

"Hurrah, boys!" Houston suddenly shouted. "Hurrah for the brave men of the Alamo!"

Houston's shout was echoed by everyone in the room, including those women who had lost men there. With eyes wet and shining, and with tear tracks on their faces, they shouted with pride at the news of the terrible price their men had extracted from Santa Anna before their own voices were forever silenced.

"General Houston," Luke went on, "Colonel Esteban Lopez is headed this way now, with at least seven hundred men under his command. How many men do you have here?"

"A little over three hundred," Houston said.

"Remember the Alamo!" someone shouted. "If one hundred and eighty-three can kill fifteen hundred Mexicans, then how many do you think we can kill?"

"Yeah!" another shouted. "Let's go get 'im, General!"

Houston looked at the ragtag assortment of men who formed his "army." They had been together for only a few days and there had been no opportunity to drill or even to organize them into commands. The defenders of the Alamo had enjoyed several weeks of preparation before the battle commenced and they were in a well-fortified position. The town of Gonzales, Houston realized, was not defendable.

"No!" Houston finally said. "We won't fight them here. We'll abandon Gonzales and fight them somewhere else."

"What?" someone shouted in dismay. "You mean we are runnin'?"

"What if the men of the Alamo had run?" another called.

"If they had obeyed my instructions and abandoned the Alamo, they would be alive today and our army would be stronger for it," Houston said.

There were a few angry mutterings and Houston held up his hands to implore the crowd to be quiet.

"Listen to me," he said. "If we vent our anger on the Mexicans in a few valiant but foolhardy battles, we will accomplish nothing. I admire the courage and patriotism of the defenders of the Alamo. But how much better would it have been for all of us if they were here with us now. I say let the Mexicans come to Gonzales. Let them find deserted houses and empty larders. Let them come on farther and deeper into Texas. The closer they come, the more vulnerable they will be."

"Why do you say that?" someone shouted.

"They will outdistance their supply lines," Luke spoke up. The others looked toward him. "You all know there is not much grass on the muddy prairies at this time of year. That means the Mexicans will have to use wagons to haul grain for their horses. We won't leave any food for the men, so they will have to bring their own. Soon, they will be low on food, low on grain, low on everything. We will be with friends who will keep us supplied. We will have the advantage."

"Listen to Colonel Calhoun," Caroline urged. "What he is saying is true."

"That woman was inside the Alamo during the siege," one of the others said. "If she's willing to go along with General Houston's idea, then I reckon I am, too."

After that, there was a general agreement that the townspeople would evacuate.

By the time the meeting was over it was dark. The people hurried toward their homes. Caroline stood in front of the tavern and looked up and down the street. She could see candles flickering in all the houses as the people hurried to pack their belongings. When Houston rode away from Gonzales, he would leave nothing behind.

He wanted to take his two six-pound cannon with

him but he was afraid that they would slow down the column. Reluctantly, he ordered his men to take the guns to the middle of the Guadalupe River and push them in.

It was nearly midnight by the time the towns-people were ready to leave. Houston had only four baggage wagons but he assigned three of them to transport civilians who had no other means of transportation.

Because of her leg, and the baby, Susanna found it more comfortable to ride in one of the wagons. Caroline, on the other hand, preferred to ride alongside Luke.

The night was cloudy and damp as the band of refugees began pouring out of Gonzales. Luke and Caroline sat astride their horses next to the road and watched the train leave. Houston rode out of the shadows of the night and stood beside them for a moment.

"It pains me to have to retreat," he told them. "But I will do whatever is necessary to prevent all future murders."

"I know it is a difficult thing to do, General," Luke said, "but it is necessary."

It began to rain shortly after they left Gonzales and it rained unceasingly for the rest of the night and throughout the next day.

The dampness made the journey miserable for soldiers and civilians alike. Houston responded to the people's complaints with blistering curses but he managed to maintain control of the crowd.

Four days after they left Gonzales, the refugees reached the Colorado River. By now their ranks had been swollen by new recruits to some six hundred in number. The river was at flood stage but they were able to get across. Once they had safely reached the other side, Houston decided that the river and his army would provide enough of a barrier to help him stand against the Mexican army, so he sent the civilians on ahead while his army made camp on the east bank of the river.

"Are you certain you don't want to go on with Susanna?" Luke asked as the civilians prepared to move on. Caroline had announced that she intended to stay with the army.

"I am certain," Caroline said.

She put her hand on Luke's shoulder and looked into his eyes. "Luke, it isn't the amount of time you have together that is important—it's how you spend that time. Whatever time you and I have left, I want us to spend it together. Please say you will not force me to go on."

Luke embraced Caroline and held her close for a long moment.

"I will not force you to go on," he said. "You may stay."

"Even if General Houston says I must go on?"

Luke smiled. "If Houston says you must go on, then you will go," he said.

"But—" Caroline started to protest and Luke put his finger on her lips to shush her.

"But," he went on, "if you must go on, then I will go with you."

Houston was not pleased that Caroline would be staying with them but he had no choice. He wanted Luke as one of his commanders and Luke informed

Houston that he would stay only if Houston would allow Caroline to stay as well. Houston finally gave in.

————

On March 21, the seven hundred men under command of Colonel Lopez arrived on the west bank of the Colorado River. The river as Houston knew it would, provided an uncrossable barrier, for Houston's men would be able to pick off the Mexican soldiers as they attempted to cross. Lopez realized that, so for five days he and his army stood their ground on one side of the river staring in frustration at the Texans on the other side.

"I had hoped to make a stand here and do battle against the Mexicans, but I dare not. This is the only force left to defend Texas. If we lose this battle, Texas will lose the war."

"General, I don't think we will lose this battle," Luke said.

"Perhaps not," Houston said. "But even if we win, what will we have accomplished? Santa Anna is not with this army. We might inflict damage on this force but, until we defeat Santa Anna, the war will go on."

Houston walked over to his saddlebag and took out a map and a cut of tobacco. He carved out a chew of tobacco and stuck it in his mouth, then began poring over the map quietly.

Luke watched him for a while and realized that Houston needed some time alone, so he walked over to join Caroline, who was sharing his encampment with him. He found her preparing a stew for their lunch.

"What did General Houston say?" Caroline asked as she worked. "When does he think the battle will take place?"

"I'm not sure there will be one," Luke said. "At least, not here."

Caroline looked around the camp. The men were all working on their weapons, talking eagerly among themselves about how many Mexicans they intended to kill once the battle began.

"What do you mean it won't be here?" Caroline asked. "Everyone says this is the perfect place for a battle. They say the river is a more formidable barrier than the walls of the Alamo."

"And so it is," Luke said. "But Santa Anna isn't with Lopez and I don't think Houston intends to commit us to battle until we have a chance at Santa Anna."

"Well, whether there is to be a battle or not, we must eat," Caroline said as she ladled the stew onto two tins and handed one of them to Luke.

"Umm," Luke said, as he took the first bite. "I have never tasted anything so delicious."

Caroline smiled. "I think that is why you agreed to let me come along with you."

"Oh, I wouldn't say that's the only reason," Luke returned with a smile.

"Colonel Calhoun, there you are, sir," one of the men called to him. "Have you heard the news? We're pullin' out! General Houston has gone yellow on us, the cur!"

"General Houston has his reasons," Luke defended.

"He better," the speaker said. "Else he's liable to

find himself lookin' for a new army, 'cause this here one's gonna fight the Mexicans iffen we have to do it without a commander."

"You'll have your fight," Luke said. "I promise you that."

"Well, iffen you promise it, I'll stick aroun' a while longer and see what's gonna happen," the man said. He held up his rifle. "Bessie here is anxious to get a few o' them Mexicans."

Chapter 21

"Did you hear?" one of the disgruntled soldiers asked the man who was slogging through the mud next to him. "Houston's got it in mind to march us all the way to the Redlands."

"Louisiana?" his companion replied.

"That's a fact," the first soldier said. "I heard he was plannin' on takin' us to Louisiana so as not to get any United States troops caught up in this here war. The thing is, I don't believe Houston has the stomach for a fight."

"That ain't true," the second man said. "Why would he keep this army together iffen he had no mind to fight?"

"I don't know why he's keepin' an army," the first man said. "And I most especial' don't know why he's makin' us march all day long in the rain like he's done."

The Texans marched for thirty miles in a driving rain without a break, finally bivouacking near the town of San Felipe on the Brazos River. Caroline was so tired that she had no difficulty sleeping, despite the fact that the tent kept out only half of the falling rain.

The next morning, before the camp was awake, Captain Baker and Captain Martin came to the tent and called to Luke. He slipped on his boots and went outside. Caroline huddled inside Luke's blanket, listening to their conversation.

"Me and Wiley Martin is decided," Caroline heard Baker say. "We ain't gonna retreat no more."

"Gentlemen, I know Sam Houston," Luke said. "Believe me, he has a reason for what he's doing."

"Maybe so," Baker said. "But I ain't goin' with him any farther and I got a hunnert n' twenty men who ain't goin' either."

"That goes for me, too," Martin added. "And the hunnert men I got."

"Gentlemen, if you pull out now, you will deplete the general's force by one-third. Is that really what you want to do?"

"No," Baker said. "I wanna fight."

"Then stay with us."

"I can't do that," Baker said. "I only come to you this mornin' so's you wouldn't think we'd skedaddled on you."

"I'm sorry you feel that way," Luke said, wearily. "But I suppose you must do what you think is right."

The two captains left then and Luke called Caroline out of the tent so they could strike camp. Shortly after the two companies took their leave from the main body, General Houston called the men together and spoke to them.

"My friends, it is not my habit to seek the counsel of others when a decision is to be made," Houston said. "A commander who does that lacks the courage to stand behind his own decisions. But there are certain rumors afoot which I feel I must put to rest. I am told that evil-disposed persons have reported that I intend to march you to the Redlands. This is false. I am going to march you into the Brazos bottom where you can whip the enemy ten to one and where we will find an abundant supply of corn."

"Now. you're talkin', General!" someone shouted.

"Ten to one!" another said. "Them's about the proper odds, I reckon."

There were other shouts and whoops and, when the meeting broke up, the mood of the soldiers had lightened considerably. Houston signaled that he wanted to talk to Luke.

"I'd say you did the right thing by telling them your plan," Luke said.

"I have some more news for them," Houston said grimly. "But I don't want to tell them just yet."

"What news is that?" Luke asked.

"It seems that at Goliad, Colonel Fannin formed a square of his wagons and equipment, and using that as his personal Alamo, attempted to stand off the Mexicans." Houston sighed. "I must give Fannin credit for more courage than I thought he possessed. He and his men fought for two days. They killed two hundred fifty Mexicans, while suffering only seven dead and sixty wounded. Then they surrendered to General Urrea on promise that they would be treated with honor and sent on parole to the United States."

Houston let out his breath, slowly. "But, on Palm Sunday, the Mexicans assembled the entire Texas force, some four hundred in all, marched them out of Goliad, lined them up, and shot them."

Luke was speechless, unable to believe his ears. "About one hundred Texans managed to get away," Houston said. "But all the wounded, including Colonel Fannin himself, were executed."

"Santa Anna is mad," Luke said. "He should be shot."

"Yes," Houston agreed. "But we dare not."

"General, what are you saying?"

"Don't you see?" Houston said. "My entire plan is based upon one thing. We must capture Santa Anna— and we must keep him alive!"

"Why? What right does he have to live?"

"He has no right," Houston said. "But he is the president of Mexico. If we capture him, we can force him to make a peace and to recognize our claim to independence."

"I suppose you're right," Luke said. "But when the men find out about Goliad, we're going to be hard-pressed to stop them from killing Santa Anna on sight."

"I know," Houston said. "That's why I have said nothing about Goliad yet."

"But they'll find out. You know they will."

"Yes, I know," Houston said. "But I want to put it off as long as I can."

Houston moved his army out shortly after that. They marched for three days through rain that scarcely broke. In the meantime, news of what had happened at Goliad traveled throughout Texas. It had the desired effect, as far as Santa Anna was concerned. The people of Texas were terrified by the behavior of the approaching Mexican Army and the civilian evacuation in the path of the army turned into a panic-driven exodus.

A scout named Noah Smithwick reported to Luke. "You listen to this 'n tell me iffen you don't think it's strange."

"They's houses standing there with the doors wide open and not hide nor hair aroun' to defend 'em against thieves. They's beds what ain't even been made, breakfast tables not cleaned off, and pans of milk moldin' in the dairies. They's cribs full of com, smokehouses full of bacon, yards full of chickens, nests of eggs, and untended gardens. Now what is it that's got folks panicked so?"

"Santa Anna," Luke answered without elaboration. Luke went to Houston with the news and Houston explained that the rumors had already begun circulating through the ranks. He decided to tell the Texans what had happened to Fannin.

"Maybe it will help me build an army," Houston said.

The Texans were outraged by what Houston reported and many were ready to turn around and go back to meet Santa Anna head on. They shouted their intention to do so but Houston held up his hands to call for quiet.

"Men, if we meet Santa Anna now, we will kill many of his men. Maybe we will even kill Santa Anna himself. But we aren't an army yet and, in the end, the overwhelming numbers of the Mexicans in the field will carry the battle. If we are defeated, there will be no more Texas. All Americans in Texas will be driven out—or worse. We have only one chance now and that is to use what time we have to become an army. We must be disciplined and we must be trained. I ask you to stay by me for a while longer until I think you are ready. Then, we will carry the fight to the enemy."

As before, Houston's eloquent oratory saved the situation and the men left the meeting determined to become a real army, the better to defeat Santa Anna.

Houston divided his army into three regiments. He gave one regiment to Luke Calhoun, another to Colonel Edward Burleson, and a third to Colonel Sidney Sherman. Then, he began training his men. He developed discipline in the ranks and he drilled them unceasingly. He kept patrols moving through the woods and scouting for several miles around his position to make certain that the Mexican Army didn't catch him unaware. Houston also used that time to get his equipment in shape. Rifles were oiled, knives were sharpened, wagons were repaired, and cannon were assembled. There was no shortage of food. The men slaughtered cattle from the pastures and took corn from the cribs of a nearby plantation. The army was divided into mess units and each unit was provided with a packhorse to carry its provisions.

There was a shortage of coffee but there was plenty of tobacco.

At first, Houston had lamented the fact that his soldiers were without uniforms but he soon discovered that his men wore their ragtag clothing like a badge of honor.

"Rags are our uniform, sir!" one of the men said proudly. "Nine out of ten of our men are in rags. And it is a fighting uniform!"

The two artillery pieces that Houston's army

assembled during this time were six-pounders supplied by the citizens of Cincinnati. The guns were a matched pair so the men quickly named them the Twin Sisters.

Houston worked longer and harder than anyone else in the entire army. Often he dozed in his saddle, so tired was he from the long hours and he claimed that those catnaps provided him with all the rest he needed.

Houston carried several ears of corn in his saddlebag and, many times, instead of taking the time to prepare a meal, he would gnaw on the raw corn. He also had two books with him, *Gulliver's Travels* and Caesar's *Commentaries*. When he did find a few spare moments, he used them to read his books or to study his maps.

Houston didn't have any liquor with him because he wanted to keep his wits about him. It was necessary that he be on his toes all the time because Santa Anna was not his only enemy. There was, brewing within his own camp, a persistent rumor of mutiny. The officers and many of the men were growing tired of the constant drilling. They wanted action and they wanted it right away. They felt that Houston's lengthy delay might be the result of a lack of courage.

Finally, Houston decided that the only way to deal with incipient mutiny was to meet it head on. He had several graves dug. Then he assembled the men and had them walk by in ranks and look down into the graves he had just opened.

"Look into them, gentlemen," he said, "for the next person who suggests a course of action contrary to the one I have laid out will be shot and buried, right here."

Houston's forceful action paid off and, though the grumbling continued, it was merely the grumbling of men who had grown tired of drilling and it had been heard from every soldier in every army that had ever drilled. Talk and plans for a mutiny were never mentioned again.

———

COLONEL LOPEZ WAITED and fumed on the west bank of the Colorado River. Just before Houston and his Texans had pulled out, an additional six hundred men had arrived, swelling Lopez's command to over thirteen hundred. With this huge force, he had planned to cross the river in two places, then converge on the Texans. He had been getting ready to strike when, suddenly, the Texans moved out.

Lopez was going to chase them when a courier arrived ordering him to stay where he was. Santa Anna was going to join Lopez's division.

The Mexican general arrived in grand style in the luxurious comfort of a liveried coach. The six prancing white horses stopped near Lopez's field headquarters and Santa Anna's face appeared in the window. As Lopez walked toward the coach, he heard a giggle from inside. He saw a girl busily adjusting the bodice of her dress. Then she sat quietly, with her hands folded in her lap, trying to regain her dignity.

"Lopez, my dear cousin," Santa Anna greeted.

"Excellency," Lopez replied, saluting. "Welcome to my headquarters."

"They are my headquarters now, Colonel," Santa Anna said. The coachman opened the door and Santa

Anna got out. He had to reach for the door frame of the coach to keep from falling over. Lopez could tell by Santa Anna's eyes that he had been using opium.

"Yes, General," Lopez said, easily, "this is your headquarters."

"Let us cross the river," Santa Anna said. "We must catch the enemy."

"Yes, General," Lopez replied. On that, he was in complete agreement. He would have crossed the river earlier had he not been ordered to wait for the president.

It took more than an hour for the army to cross the river. When they reached the other side, they went at once to San Felipe, reaching the village on April 7. But when they arrived, they discovered that the town no longer existed. It had been abandoned and burned to the ground.

———

CAPTAIN BAKER, who had left Houston's army because he refused to retreat, had burned the town and he and his men were waiting for the Mexicans on the opposite side of the Brazos River. They had taken every boat with them to delay the Mexicans' crossing. Santa Anna ordered that rafts be built.

Baker's riflemen were well dug in, and their deadly accurate fire kept the Mexicans from crossing the Brazos for four days.

Santa Anna grew impatient with the drawn-out fight so he ordered Lopez and seven-hundred-fifty of his men to come south with him to the crossing at Fort Bend. The fort, his scouts had reported, was abandoned and they could cross there quickly and easily.

There was a tavern in Fort Bend owned by a woman named Elizabeth Powell. She had refused to abandon her tavern for fear it would be destroyed. As a result, she was standing in the doorway when Santa Anna arrived on horseback. Santa Anna took over the tavern for himself and his officers and ordered Mrs. Powell to serve dinner.

That night, as Mrs. Powell and her son served the meal, Santa Anna and his officers sat around the table eating and discussing strategy.

"General, do you not think it would be wise to save our discussion until after our meal?" Lopez asked. "Suppose this woman and her son overhear us and send word of our plans?"

"Nonsense," Santa Anna answered. "This woman speaks no Spanish." He turned to the woman, who was at that moment serving beans. "Tell me, woman, do you speak Spanish?" he demanded.

"I'm sorry, sir, but if you want something you will have to speak in English," the woman answered.

Santa Anna chuckled and held up his glass. "You see," he said to Lopez. "She understands nothing."

The woman refilled Santa Anna's glass, then returned to the kitchen, but she left the door open just a crack.

"Gentlemen," Santa Anna went on, "my scouts have told me that Sam Houston is just upriver from San Felipe. Houston is teaching his Texans how to be an army. As if these backwoodsmen could be taught such a skill."

Santa Anna laughed at the statement.

"Forgive me, General, but the backwoodsmen who defended the Alamo did quite well for themselves," Lopez reminded Santa Anna.

"They were desperate men, driven to desperate acts," Santa Anna said. "On an open field of battle, we would have dispatched them even more quickly."

"General, is it your intention to strike at Houston?" one of the officers asked.

"We could attack Houston, yes, but I have a better idea," Santa Anna said. He leaned forward on the table and smiled. "While Houston trains his men, we will proceed to Harrisburg."

"What is at Harrisburg?"

Santa Anna smiled again. "The so-called government of Texas. We will strike there, capture the leaders of this rebel force, then turn north to crush Sam Houston."

"A brilliant plan."

"Yes," Santa Anna said. "We will proceed at first light."

"General, wouldn't it be better to move the troops up tonight?" Lopez asked.

"No," Santa Anna said. "I have other plans for tonight and her name is Emily."

There was a ripple of ribald laughter around the table. As the officers reached for more food, they didn't notice the door to the kitchen being softly closed.

"Tim," Mrs. Powell called softly to her son, summoning him to her "Yes, Mama?"

"Slip out the back way. Get word to Sam Houston that Santa Anna is planning to seize the government at Harrisburg."

"Yes, Mama," Tim said.

"Here," Mrs. Powell said, giving him a bucket. "Act as if you are going for water. When you are out of sight, slip away."

Tim walked nonchalantly through the Mexican troops and down to the riverbank. When he was out of sight, he began to run along the river. He reached Houston's camp at dawn the next day.

When Tim was taken to Houston's tent, the general was talking with a civilian named Donoho, who had complained that Houston's men were stripping his timber for firewood.

"Mr. Donoho, so far nearly one thousand men have given their lives, thousands more have given their time, and many have donated money, arms, food, and equipment to this war. Is it too much to ask that you allow a few hundred men to use some of your firewood?"

"The wood belongs to me," Donoho insisted. "You and your men have no right to it."

"Sergeant Collins," Houston called.

"Yes, sir?"

"Is it true that our men are cutting firewood from Mr. Donoho's land?"

"Yes, sir," the sergeant replied. He spit out a stream of tobacco juice.

"General, we got to get it somewhere."

"Why are you cutting his timber," Houston asked, "when he has already split rails for his fence? Wouldn't that be a lot easier?"

"What?" Donoho gasped.

Sergeant Collins smiled broadly.

"Yes, sir General, I reckon that would be a whole heap easier," he said.

"No!" Donoho shouted. "Tell your men they can cut from my timber. As much as they want."

"I thought you might see things my way," Houston said.

Shaking his head in frustration, Donoho left the area. Houston turned toward young Tim Powell, who was bathed in sweat from his long run.

"What is this?" he asked.

"This boy ran all the way here from Fort Bend," a soldier explained.

"You must have important news," Houston said.

"Yes, sir," Tim said. "At least, my mama thinks so. Santa Anna and his army spent the night at our place. Mama, she speaks Spanish, only she let on like she didn't, and she heard 'em makin' their plans. General Houston, Santa Anna is gonna move north and try to capture our government."

Houston grinned broadly and slammed his fist into his hand.

"All right," he said. "This is what we have been waiting for Tim, you did well."

"General, can I serve in your army?"

"Ain't you a little young?" Sergeant Collins asked.

"Sergeant, anyone who can be trusted to do what this young man did tonight is welcome to serve in my army. Issue him a rifle."

Tim smiled broadly. "Now we'll get 'em."

Chapter 22

The Mexican Army discovered that the Texas government had fled town. Everyone had left except the staff of *The Telegraph and Texas Register*, the local newspaper. The newspapermen told Lopez that President Burnet and the other officials of the Texas government had escaped to New Washington aboard the steamer *Cayuga*.

Lopez took the news to Santa Anna. At first, the general was angry. Then they looked at a map. It would take the steamer some time to reach New Washington, because of the meanderings of the river. But by land, New Washington was only twenty miles away.

Santa Anna made plans to take his entire army there when he learned that Houston was going to defend Lynch's Ferry, a point about fifteen miles east of Harrisburg. The information pleased Santa Anna because now he believed he could capture the Texas government and deal with Houston's army all at the same time.

"Now, we will put an end to this foolishness—once and for all," he said. He looked around the town of Harrisburg. Like the other towns, it was deserted. But, unlike the others, it had not been burned to the ground.

"It looks to me as if the Texans were careless," Santa Anna said. "They forgot to burn the town."

"There was no need," Lopez said. "I've already had my men search. There is nothing here we can use."

"Burn it," Santa Anna said. "Burn every last stick."

Lopez delivered the order and, within a short while, every building in town blazed brightly and smoke boiled into the sky.

———

"WHAT IS THAT SMOKE?" Caroline asked as she rode beside Luke.

Luke looked in the direction indicated by Caroline and saw a wisp of smoke on the horizon. The wisp was small but it was so far away that Luke realized it must be a big fire.

"Harrisburg," he said. "Harrisburg is burning."

"Who burned it?" Caroline asked. "Texans or Americans?"

"Ah," Luke said, holding his finger up. "That is, indeed, the question."

For the rest of the day, Houston's troops continued to march toward Harrisburg. Their spirits were high because they were certain they would soon meet Santa Anna.

———

Lopez was at the head of the dragoons, the advance party of Santa Anna's troops. As they approached New Washington, where he hoped to capture President Burnet and the other government officials, Lopez spotted an American scout. The scout saw the Mexicans and turned back toward the town at a gallop.

"Stop him!" Lopez shouted. "Catch him before he can give a warning!"

Three of the fastest riders broke out of the ranks and gave chase but Lopez knew the American was going to get away. He had too much of a head start. There was one thing he could do, however. He could move the entire company at a gallop. Perhaps they could arrive so closely on the scout's heels that no one would have time to react to his warning. Lopez stood in his stirrups and urged his men forward at a gallop.

The trees along each side of the road echoed the thunder of the hoof beats as the fifty horsemen pounded toward the town of New Washington. They entered the town without breaking stride and Lopez led them to the docks. There was a schooner in the harbor and Lopez saw a rowboat approaching it. President Burnet sat in the rowboat, along with several others. Some of the Mexicans raised their rifles and took aim but then Lopez saw a woman in the boat with the men.

"No!" he shouted. "Don't fire! There's a woman in the boat!"

Lopez's men lowered their weapons and the boat continued to row out to the schooner. Once on board the schooner, the Texas government was safe.

Santa Anna arrived in New Washington a while later. He was annoyed by the escape of President

Burnet but not too concerned about it. His primary mission, he believed, was to defeat Sam Houston. Once Houston was taken care of, the government of Texas would fall into his hands like a ripe plum.

"General, perhaps we should leave now," Lopez suggested. "If we made haste, we might reach Lynch's Ferry ahead of Houston. We could ambush him there."

"There is no need to hurry," Santa Anna insisted. "Victory is within our grasp and I desire a short rest. I saw a plantation near here. Does anyone know what it is called?"

"It is Morgan's plantation, General," one of his staff officers informed him.

"Does this plantation have slaves?" Santa Anna asked.

"Yes, General."

Santa Anna smiled. "Ah, good. I have grown tired of the women who are with us. I shall require someone new for a small diversion. As soon as we are there, you will bring me the loveliest slave girls. I will make my choice. Oh, and see to it that my opium box is well filled."

"Yes, General," the staff officer said.

Lopez stood quietly until Santa Anna moved on.

"That hedonistic fool is going to lose this war," Lopez said quietly. "And this is a war that could be lost only by someone with Santa Anna's genius for catastrophe."

———

AFTER TWO AND a half days of forced marching, Caroline, Luke, and the others with General Houston reached Buffalo Bayou, just across from Harrisburg.

Caroline looked across the water "You were right," she said. "It *was* Harrisburg that burned."

The town lay in heaps and piles of black and gray ashes. A dog, lonely and afraid, picked its way among the ash piles as if trying to find its former home.

"Damn!" Houston swore. He had ridden his horse over to stand beside Caroline and Luke, as they stared at the remains of the town. "We missed Santa Anna. Where is he?"

"General, look what we've got!" someone shouted.

Houston, Luke, and Caroline turned toward the voice. A dozen men were shoving a Mexican along in front of them. The Mexican was in uniform and he was shaking with fear.

"This here fella is a courier," one of the men said.

"A courier you say?" Houston replied. "Well, now, maybe we're about to get a break." Houston swung down from his horse and confronted the courier. "What messages are you carrying?"

"Here's his saddlebag," one of the men shouted. He started to pass the bag to Houston, then suddenly stopped and stared at it.

"You son of a bitch!" he shouted at the courier. "You bastard, I ought to kill you myself!"

"What is it?" someone else called.

"Look at the name on this saddlebag," the Texan said. "William Barret Travis!"

"Kill him!" someone else shouted. "Kill the Mexican son of a bitch!"

"No!" Houston said, holding up his hands. "Let us not descend to the level of the people we are fighting."

"But he was at the Alamo," someone protested.

"They were all at the Alamo," Houston replied. "We will not kill him. Give me the messages. Let's see what we can find out."

The messages were from Fort Bend and they were directed to Santa Anna. From them, Houston learned that Santa Anna had split his forces into three divisions and that he was in New Washington with only seven hundred-fifty men—not many more men than Houston had with him. For the first time in this war, the Texans were to meet the Mexicans in equal numbers.

Houston also learned from the messages, however, that five hundred reinforcements would soon join Santa Anna at Lynch's Ferry, about eight miles away from New Washington on the plain of San Jacinto.

After Houston digested all the information, he climbed back onto his big white stallion and called for his army to gather around him.

"The time has come!" he said. "You have been waiting for battle and it is about to be thrust upon us. Victory is certain! Trust in God and fear not! The victims of the Alamo and those who were murdered at Goliad cry out for vengeance. Remember the Alamo! Remember Goliad!"

"Remember the Alamo!" someone called back and his shout was echoed by everyone present.

"Remember Goliad!"

Again, the stirring call to battle was answered.

"They are ready to fight, General," Luke said as the formation broke up.

"I *hope* they're ready." Houston cut a plug of tobacco and put it in his mouth. "Battle is pressed upon us now, Colonel Calhoun," Houston said. "This is our only chance to save Texas. We must win. If we lose, it will be all over."

"When will we move?" Luke asked.

"At once. Put the men to building rafts. We shall cross the bayou tonight and move toward Harrisburg in the dark. It is my hope that we can get there before the Mexicans expect us."

The troops spent the rest of the afternoon building rafts. Then they began ferrying men across the bayou. Houston tore his pants on a nail, made some joke about it, and the men laughed.

"They are in good spirits," Caroline said.

"Yes," Luke agreed. "They sense a victory."

"Luke, will we be victorious?" Caroline asked, anxiously.

"We have to be," Luke replied though Caroline realized that he hadn't actually answered her question.

Caroline and Luke crossed on a raft with the others. When the entire army was across, they started toward Lynch's Ferry, some thirteen miles away.

———

WHILE THE REST of Houston's army marched through the night to Lynch's Ferry, Don Esteban Lopez prepared to spend that night as a "guest" at Morgan's plantation.

Santa Anna occupied the big house, Lopez was given a cabin. The next morning, Lopez stepped onto the front porch of the little cabin. The great house was about fifty yards away, on the other side of an open ditch. There were hundreds of tents pitched about on the plantation grounds and the occupants of the tents were just awakening, testing gingerly the world they had abandoned the night before.

It was very early in the morning and, though there was light, the sun had not yet risen above the surrounding trees. The men went about their morning routine—shaving, relieving themselves in the ditch, starting their breakfast fires.

A rooster crowed.

Lopez left the porch and walked among the tents to the big house. A guard came to attention as he pushed the door open to go inside.

An American and his wife sat fearfully on a sofa in the parlor as Lopez went in and they looked at him with frightened eyes. Lopez knew that the Morgans feared for their lives. He wanted to tell them not to be afraid but he honestly didn't know what whim would dictate Santa Anna's behavior. He would not have thought the survivors of Goliad would be murdered but Santa Anna had done just that.

There was a burst of laughter from the dining room and Lopez went toward the sound.

"Ah, Don Esteban," Santa Anna greeted. "I hoped you would join us for breakfast."

There were half a dozen other senior officers with Santa Anna.

"We are having quail and eggs. A wonderful breakfast for the day of a battle, don't you think?"

"Do you believe we will do battle today, General?" Lopez asked. He sat down and, almost instantly, food appeared before him.

"Yes," Santa Anna said. "I think this will be our lucky day. We will be at Lynch's Ferry when Houston arrives and we will give him a surprise welcome."

"What if he is already there when we arrive?" Lopez asked.

"That is impossible," Santa Anna said. "His army —" Santa Anna slurred the word— "is on foot. They couldn't possibly be at Lynch's Ferry yet."

"I wish I had your confidence, Your Excellency," Lopez said.

"We will be victorious this day," Santa Anna said, smiling patronizingly at Lopez. "I am willing to stake my position on it."

"Mr. President, you are doing just that," Lopez reminded him.

Chapter 23

The bulk of Houston's army had spent what was left of the night in a protective copse of trees, south of Buffalo Bayou. They had arrived just before dawn, taken control of Lynch's Ferry, then moved across the bayou to rest and wait. They didn't rest unprotected, however. Houston had sent out a patrol.

The patrol returned and informed Houston that Santa Anna and his men were bivouacked on the Morgan plantation just outside New Washington. Santa Anna had burned New Washington, they said, and their report was confirmed by the smoke that curled into the sky from the little town eight miles away.

Luke had tried to persuade Caroline to wait for him across the San Jacinto River in the little village of Lynchburg but she insisted on coming across with him.

"I survived the Alamo," she told him. "What could be worse than that?"

"You were spared at the Alamo," Luke said. "If we lose this battle, you may not be spared a second time."

"For a while, those of us who were left alive at the Alamo envied the dead. I will stay with you."

"Then you must promise me that when the battle begins, you will stay back in the woods, out of danger. Without the assurance of your safety, I will not be able to fight."

"I promise I'll stay out of harm's way."

The woods in which the Texans were now resting, and in which Caroline promised to stay out of danger, were thick with oak trees from which hung tangled strands of Spanish moss. These woods lined Buffalo Bayou which the Texans had crossed before capturing Lynch's Ferry. The ferry itself crossed the San Jacinto River. Alongside the river ran woods and marshland. About a mile downstream, the river formed a small backwater basin known as Peggy Lake. The lake protruded at a right angle from the river and it, too, was surrounded by marsh and woods. The result was a great plain almost completely encircled by woods. The field was called the San Jacinto Plain.

The Texans rested and waited as the Mexicans moved toward them. Santa Anna was determined to arrive there first, establish a strong position, and ambush Houston when the Texans arrived. He was surprised and dismayed when his scouts told him they had already spotted the Texans.

"Surely they must be long-range patrols," Santa Anna mused.

"I don't think so," Lopez said. "I think Houston has beaten us to the ferry."

"Quickly," Santa Anna said, "have your men take

up positions in the wood line on this side of the field. The Texans won't come across the plain after us. As soon as General Cos gets here with his division, we shall have enough strength to go after the devil."

Santa Anna moved his soldiers into the woods. Then he ordered them to haul the lone cannon into position.

"We'll show the Americans that not even the woods are safe from our artillery," he said to the battery commander. The men set up the gun, loaded it, and then fired. Santa Anna pranced forward on his white stallion, ordering his gunners to load and fire again. Suddenly, there was a whistling noise. Then a cannonball crashed through the trees. It felled half a dozen Mexican dragoons and the thunder of artillery fire rolled across the plains.

The Texans had artillery too! That realization surprised and unnerved Santa Anna and, quickly, he retired from the scene.

"HA! YOU GOT A BUNCH OF 'EM!" a soldier shouted from his post high in one of the trees near the Twin Sisters cannon.

The lookout clung precariously to his perch with one hand, while with the other, holding a spyglass to his eye. He called down to the gun crews, "I see five— no, six! There's six Mexicans down."

The men around the guns cheered.

"That was a lucky shot," Luke said.

"Luck?" the battery commander answered. He patted the breech of the gun. "Colonel, luck has nothing to do with it. That was pure skill. We are an army now. A real army."

Luke smiled. "I see. And you believe that artillery makes us an army?"

"Certainly. Artillery lends dignity to what would otherwise be a bloody brawl," the gun commander said.

Luke laughed.

The heavy guns exchanged fire a few more times. Then, Houston ordered the Twin Sisters to stop firing in order to preserve powder. The Mexicans stopped firing their cannon but they kept up their brisk musket fire throughout the rest of the day. They were far out of range, however, and not one ball reached the Texas lines.

The Texans began complaining again. They had been prepared for battle but as the day wore on, it began to look as if Houston had no intention of engaging Santa Anna.

They satisfied themselves by saying that there would be an attack at first light and they made all preparations for battle before they went to sleep that night.

Santa Anna also believed that Houston would attack with first light and he spent the entire night fortifying his position. While the Texans slept, the Mexicans worked— erecting barricades, packing supplies, and digging trenches. Even Santa Anna stayed awake, hurrying from one position to another, giving contradictory orders as to how he wanted the barricades to be built. He grew more and more irritable as the night wore on and, more than once, he threatened to have men shot for not responding quickly enough to his orders.

When the sun came up the next morning, the Texans awoke, anxious to attack. They soon learned, however, that Houston had left word not to be awakened until eight o'clock. It was his first sound sleep in many days.

The Texans looked at one another dejectedly and grumbled among themselves. Some wondered if Houston was ever going to fight.

Luke had led a morning scouting patrol and now he returned to the Texas camp with news. He had seen General Cos' men coming from the direction of Harrisburg. Cos had moved up during the night and, within the hour, he would join Santa Anna.

Houston took the news without comment. Then he ate his breakfast in a surprisingly good mood.

"That's good news about General Cos," he said to Luke and the others.

"Good news? But it nearly doubles Santa Anna's strength."

"It is better for Cos to arrive now, before the battle, than to get here in the middle of the fighting. At least there will be no unpleasant surprises for us."

"General, for a cautious man, you seem in excellent spirits this morning," Luke observed.

Houston chuckled. "And so I am, Colonel Calhoun. I saw an eagle this morning. That's always a good sign, you know."

"No, I didn't know," Luke answered with a smile.

"Come," Houston said, "let's move among the men." Luke followed Houston through the Texas camp. The men rested around several campfires and the smoke from the fires hung low in the air. Sunshine stabbed down through the twisted growth of trees and the rays of light were alive with drifting smoke.

"Boys," Houston called out to them, "are you ready for a fight?"

"Yes!" the men shouted back.

"Well, enjoy your dinners, boys. Eat hearty and then I will lead you into a fight. And if you whip them, every one of you shall be a captain."

"Hurrah, boys, hurrah!" someone shouted and the shout traveled as an echo through the woods.

"Luke, I want you to take some men with you and destroy Vince's Bridge."

"Destroy it, General?" one of the other officers said.

"Yes," Houston replied. "I don't want any more Mexican reinforcements to arrive during the battle."

"But, General, if we do that, we won't have any means of escape, should retreat become necessary."

"True," Houston said. "That leaves us only two alternatives: victory or death."

"I'll take care of the bridge, General," Luke said.

"Colonel Calhoun," Houston called after him, "unless you hasten back, you will find this prairie changed from green to red by the time you return."

Shortly after the noon meal, Houston assembled all his officers. He looked around at the men who had been grumbling for the last several weeks because Houston had chosen not to fight.

"The time has come," Houston said. "I have delayed fighting so long that some of you have questioned my courage. Despite your accusations, I put off fighting because I was waiting for this moment. Gentlemen, the history of Texas hinges on the fighting we engage in today. Shall this great territory become a vassal state to the Mexicans or shall we take control of our own destiny and breathe the air of free men? That question will be resolved here today. This is not just a battle, gentlemen. This is the entire war! The only question remaining is this. Shall we attack the enemy or wait to receive their attack?"

When Houston posed that question, the officers began arguing among themselves, trying to arrive at the best answer. The consensus was that it would be too risky to attack across an open field. The Texans would dig in and wait for the Mexicans to attack them.

Houston laughed. "Thank you, gentlemen, for your words of wisdom and *courage*," he teased.

At a little after three o'clock that afternoon, Luke returned with words that the bridge had been destroyed.

"Excellent," Houston said. He looked up at the sky. The sun was high and warm though there was a light breeze.

"Luke, do you feel like fighting?"

"That I do, General."

"Well, then, let us go."

Word was passed to all the officers and the army was soon under arms and ready to go. They spread out in two rows over the field, nearly a thousand yards across. Luke was in the middle of the first row.

A mile away across the knee-high grass, the Mexicans waited in their camp. Texan lookouts, high in the trees, had already reported that the Mexicans had no patrols working and no sentries in sight. In fact, most of the Mexicans, exhausted from their all-night activity, were asleep. Their guns were neatly stacked while the soldiers dozed in the warm afternoon sun.

Santa Anna was himself asleep and, though he, too, had worked during the night, his sleep was deepened by opium as well as fatigue.

On the Texas side of the field, Houston rode silently along the two rows of men. When he reached the center, he stopped in front of Luke, then rode thirty yards forward.

"The general's not gonna stay up there durin' the attack, is he?" someone asked.

"Lord, I hope not. Why, he's the first one, them Mex riflemen would shoot at."

"And he'd make a dandy target on that big white stallion," another added.

"Trail arms," Houston called out in a firm voice.

The soldiers lifted their rifles.

"Forward!" Houston called.

———

CAROLINE WATCHED the Texans start across the field. She waited until they were some distance away, then turned to go into the woods behind her.

A big hospital tent stood nearby. Inside it, several men were working diligently, preparing to receive the wounded. Caroline recognized one officer as the division surgeon. Behind him stood three sturdy tables. On each table, the men had placed a knife and a saw. Soldiers were busily rolling bandages and stocking them near the tables. Caroline knew they were preparing for amputations and the sight made her feel queasy. She leaned against a tree and looked away.

"We have to get ready for 'em, Miss Lafont," the surgeon explained.

"I know," Caroline said. "Forgive me. I was just being weak."

"I reckon we all are at one time or another," the surgeon replied. '

Caroline turned back toward the open field. The men who were marching across it had grown small in the distance. The ground was soft from the heavy rain and deep furrows stretched out in long lines, pointing to the cannon that were being pulled toward the battleground. There was absolute silence and, now, even the jangle of equipment and tramp of feet was muffled.

Somewhere a woodpecker drummed impatiently—the only sound heard.

"Why aren't they playing the fife and drums?" Caroline asked.

"When you hear that, you'll know they've been discovered," the surgeon said. "The sound of gunfire will come soon after that."

The sound of drums and fife reached them a moment later and Caroline took a deep breath and said a short prayer.

———

"BRING THE CANNONS FORWARD," Houston ordered and the men rolled the Twin Sisters ahead of the line and into position. The gun crews poured in powder, then wadding, and then cannonballs. They looked at Houston and he brought down his battered campaign hat in a grand, sweeping gesture. Both guns roared as one and the deathly silence was ended.

As soon as the men fired the guns, the Texans started running toward the barricades.

"Remember the Alamo!" someone shouted.

"Remember Goliad!" another returned.

"Remember the Alamo!" still another said, and that became the battle cry on every Texan's tongue as the angry men surged forward. *"Remember the Alamo!"*

"My God!" Lopez shouted when he saw the Texans charging toward them. "Bugler, sound the alarm!"

The bugler stood up and looked toward the Texans. His lips were trembling so that he could scarcely blow a clear note.

"Sound it!" Lopez ordered angrily. "You were willing enough to sound the death knell at the Alamo, now blow the alarm!"

The bugler finally sounded his call and the Mexican soldiers who had been asleep awoke from their dreams in total confusion.

Houston tried to get the Texans to halt and fire, but they were too angry and too intent on closing with the enemy. They continued to charge toward the Mexican lines.

"Colonel Calhoun!" Houston called out. "They must stop and fire now! If the Mexicans are waiting for us, they will cut us down like hay!"

Luke, like Houston, tried to get the Texans to halt and fire, but they would not respond. They continued to press forward, shouting "Alamo," over and over again.

Finally, when the Texans were no more than sixty yards from the Mexicans, they loosed their first volley of musket fire. They reloaded immediately and pressed on with the attack.

The men of the second line had moved forward to merge with the first and now the single rank of attackers was fifteen hundred yards long. The orderly precision had ended and the Texans were charging the Mexicans at a dead run.

Houston's horse was shot out from under him and he stepped off skillfully as it went down. There were, however, many riderless horses running panic-stricken across the battlefield and Houston managed to catch one of them and swing into the saddle.

Moments after getting on his second horse, Houston was struck in the ankle by a ball and that horse went down as well. Houston mounted a third horse and galloped forward to join his men, who had broken through the Mexican barricades.

The Mexicans were now in a total panic. Many had never had the chance to retrieve their weapons. They were running around among the trees or out onto the plain, fair game for the Texans.

The attackers shot, clubbed, and knifed the enemy soldiers at will. Every Texan seemed to feel a blood lust and no one thought of his personal safety but only of avenging those who had died at the Alamo and Goliad. Hatred for the Mexicans poured forth in the slaughter that ensued. Even Houston joined in. His boot was filled with blood from his wound but, despite his pain, he rode forward, slashing Mexican soldiers with his sabre.

One group of Mexicans put up a spirited defense and Luke, suddenly, found himself surrounded by four of them. He shot one man and saw the others smile, thinking he had exhausted his one charge. They didn't know about the magnificent pistol Luke had and he squeezed off three more rounds, killing all four of them.

Lopez was fighting for his life when he saw Santa Anna running away. "Come back here, you coward!" Lopez shouted.

Santa Anna didn't react to Lopez's shout. He leaped on the back of a horse and rode away, leaving his men to die under the vengeful wrath of the Texans.

The actual battle was decided less than twenty minutes after the Twin Sisters loosed their first barrage. Then the killing came to an end and the Texans stood in silence, surveying the carnage.

A small bayou ran behind the enemy camp and the Mexican soldiers who had tried to cross it had been trapped there. The bayou was choked with their bodies and the water, red with blood, began to surge through the grisly dam.

With the battle won, Houston turned and rode back across the plain to his headquarters.

Luke, who had led the attack on foot, now commandeered a Mexican horse and rode back with General Houston, steadying his commander in the saddle. Houston's wound was painful and had cost him a great loss of blood which had weakened him considerably.

Caroline was waiting anxiously for the men to return and she recognized Luke long before he was close. She let out a cry of joy and ran to meet him. She walked along beside him, holding onto the saddle pommel.

"For God's sake, man," Houston said, his voice

strained with pain. "Pick her up and let her ride with you. That's no way for a gentleman to treat a lady."

Luke laughed and stretched out his arm. Caroline swung up onto the horse behind him, put her arms around him, and squeezed him tightly. The battle was over and Luke was unharmed.

When they reached the Texas camp, Luke had the doctor look at Houston. The wound was very deep and, for a while, the doctor contemplated amputating his foot. Houston refused to let them do it, insisting that they bandage the wound and let him rest. Reluctantly, they did so but they expressed their concern that he would develop gangrene.

After Houston had received treatment, he lay down beneath a tree and listened to the final report of the fighting. The battle had succeeded beyond Houston's expectations.

Eight Texans had been killed and twenty-three wounded. Six hundred Mexicans had died and the Texans had taken six hundred fifty prisoners.

But Santa Anna had escaped.

It had all been for nothing.

Chapter 24

Lopez had fought until there was nothing left for him to do but try to get away. The killing was still going on when he managed to slip through the wood line and make his escape. He mounted a riderless horse and rode quickly until the battlefield was far behind him. When he was far enough away, he walked the horse to let it rest. That was when he recognized Santa Anna's horse, tied to a tree. Slowly, he walked over toward the horse.

"Who is there?" a frightened voice called from the tall grass next to a bayou. Lopez recognized Santa Anna's voice.

"So, my cousin, here you are," Lopez said.

Santa Anna rose up and Lopez saw that he was covered with mud from hiding. He had discarded his grand tunic.

"Lopez! Thank God one of my commanders has had the sense to join me."

"Night will soon fall," Lopez announced. "Can you find your way in the dark?"

"No," Santa Anna admitted.

"Neither can I," Lopez said. "I think we should rest through the night. We can leave at first light."

Lopez and Santa Anna spent the night in a deserted house. Lopez slept lightly while Santa Anna whimpered and complained that, without his opium, he couldn't sleep well.

The next morning, just after they got under way, they discovered a dead Mexican private.

"Good!" Santa Anna said, excitedly.

"Good? This is one of our men," Lopez said.

"Yes, and even in death he shall serve his president." Santa Anna removed the soldier's tunic and put it on over his own expensive linen shirt.

"General, if you are going to wear a private's tunic, then you should wear a private's shirt as well," Lopez suggested.

"They won't look beneath the tunic," Santa Anna said. "To anyone who sees me now, I am merely a private, of no consequence."

Lopez looked at the dead private from whom Santa Anna had stripped the tunic. "Every man is of some consequence to someone," he said. "Even if only to himself."

"Come, let's go," Santa Anna ordered impatiently.

"General, if we go that way, we will encounter the Texans once more."

"No," Santa Anna insisted. "Do you think I don't know where to go? I am, remember, the hero of Tampico."

"Yes," Lopez said. "I remember."

"We will go this way," Santa Anna insisted.

Lopez knew it was the wrong way but he was,

suddenly, tired. Let the Texans capture them. Maybe it would end the war, the killing, and the despotic rule of his mad cousin.

Lopez followed Santa Anna and they soon were captured by a Texas patrol.

The Texans could tell immediately that Santa Anna, despite his private's tunic, was a man of high rank. They knew that by the way he treated Lopez, who made no attempt to conceal his rank. Then, when the soldiers took their captives to the compound where the other prisoners were being held, the Mexicans rose to their feet and cried out: "El Presidente!"

"My God," one of the captors said, "this here son of a bitch is Santa Anna hisself."

They took their prisoner to Houston.

Caroline was tending to the fire when the men led Santa Anna past. She had seen him inside the Alamo after the battle so she recognized him and called out to Luke, who was resting inside the tent. "Luke, they have Santa Anna!"

"What did you say?" Luke asked, coming quickly to the tent opening.

"They have Santa Anna," Caroline said. "I just saw him go by."

Luke came out of the tent and embraced Caroline. "This is what Houston wanted. With Santa Anna, we can sue for peace!"

"They got Santa Anna!" someone shouted. "They're takin' 'im to see the general!"

"Kill the bastard!"

"Yeah, murder the son of a bitch! What's he doin' still alive?"

"No, he must be kept alive!" Luke yelled. "If he's

killed, all our fighting will have been for nothing!"
Luke decided to walk along with Santa Anna to
protect him. As he caught up with the patrol, he recognized the Mexican officer who was with Santa Anna.

"So, Colonel Calhoun, we meet again," Lopez said.
"And under circumstances decidedly more advanta-
geous to you."

"Colonel Lopez," Luke said, "I see you have
survived."

"Thus far," Lopez said. "I have no idea what fate
awaits me. I don't suppose you do?"

"I'm afraid not," Luke said.

The men walked over to the shady spot where
Houston lay resting. His leg was bandaged and
slightly elevated.

Santa Anna stopped, clicked his heels and bowed
his head slightly. "Señor Houston, I am General Santa
Anna, president of the Republic of Mexico. I am your
prisoner, sir."

"I've got a rope here, General! You give the word
'n' I'll stretch his neck all the way back to Mexico!"

Santa Anna began to tremble. "Please," he said.
"When I was captured, your men took my medicine
box. I would like my medicine."

"Get his medicine," Houston ordered.

A moment later a small, jeweled box was pressed
into Santa Anna's hand and he took a bit of opium.
After that, he seemed better able to cope with the situation facing him.

"Have a seat," Houston said, pointing to an empty
ammunition box.

Santa Anna sat down and looked at Houston.
"May I tell you, sir, that a man may consider himself

born to no common destiny who has conquered the Napoleon of the West."

"Is that what you are?" Houston asked, unimpressed with the grandiloquence of the statement.

"Yes," Santa Anna answered. "And now it remains for you to be generous to the vanquished."

"You should have remembered that at the Alamo," Houston said quietly.

"You are a commander, sir, and a brilliant one," Santa Anna said. "You understand the rules of war. I was justified in my action at the Alamo because the defenders refused to surrender."

"You have not the same excuse for the massacre of Colonel Fannin's command," Houston roared angrily. "They surrendered on terms your general offered. And yet, after their defeat and surrender, they were all murdered."

Santa Anna began trembling again.

"Tell me, General Houston, do you intend to exact the same revenge?"

"No," Houston answered.

"General, ain't you gonna kill this son of a bitch?" one of the Texans asked.

"Not if he does as I ask," Houston said.

"And what is your demand?" Santa Anna asked.

"I want you to call an end to the fighting," Houston said. "And I want you to acknowledge our independence."

"I—I can't do that," Santa Anna protested.

"You will do it," Houston insisted. "Or I will allow my men to have their way with you."

"Let me have 'im!" someone shouted. "I lost a son-in-law in the Alamo!"

"I'll do it!" Santa Anna said quickly.

"Colonel Calhoun," Houston said, turning to Luke. "Bring General Santa Anna paper and a pen."

When the writing materials appeared, Santa Anna wrote the lines dictated by Houston. He concluded with the note: "I have agreed with General Houston upon an armistice which may put an end to the war forever."

"Now," Houston said, "I need someone to carry this note to the enemy."

"I will," Luke said.

"You'll need a Mexican officer to go with you, to verify that the note is authentic."

"Will you go with me, Colonel Lopez?" Luke asked.

Lopez smiled. "I would deem it an honor."

"General, I'd like to take Colonel Burleson and Caroline as well," Luke said. "Colonel Burleson to bring you news of the Mexican's compliance with your demand and Caroline because we have business to attend to and I don't plan to return."

Houston grabbed Luke's hand and clasped it tightly in his own.

"My boy, all Texas owes you a debt!" Houston said.

"No, General," Luke replied. "It is you to whom Texas is indebted. And Texas will never forget. Someday there will be a great city named for you and it will rival Washington in size and importance."

"Houston?" Houston replied. He laughed. "If Texas ever has a town named Houston, I predict it won't amount to much."

Chapter 25

Marlene Lafont was saddened by the news her daughter brought her of the death of her husband inside the Alamo. But she was proud, too, for news of the brave defense of the Alamo had spread throughout the United States.

Marlene was also proud to meet her new son-in-law, himself a hero of the Texas War for Independence. When Luke and Caroline returned to New Orleans as husband and wife, the whole city turned out to welcome them.

Frank Sweeny was there as well and he welcomed them with a greasy smile and a limp handshake. "By confirming your father's death," he said, "you have placed all our joint holdings in my hands alone. However, I shall be generous and offer you compensation. After all, I can't be so cruel as to turn out the family of a war hero, now, can I?"

"I'm sure your offer will be most generous," Caroline said. "Meet us at the New Orleans National Bank at two this afternoon."

Frank Sweeny rubbed his hands together eagerly. "Yes, we will conclude the arrangements then. After I buy you out, I suppose you will return to Texas?"

"I will," Caroline said. "My husband and I own a ranch there."

"Your mother and your sisters?"

"They will stay here."

"But surely, without a home, they will have no wish to stay?" Frank said.

"I'm sure they'll have a place to stay," Caroline said.

She enjoyed playing cat and mouse with Frank Sweeny and, when two o'clock came, she, her mother, her two sisters, and Luke were waiting for Sweeny at the bank. Luke had come along only to provide moral support. This maneuver was entirely in Caroline's hands and he meant to let her enjoy it to its utmost.

Simon Newcomb, the president of the bank, had been a friend of Caroline's father. Like everyone else in New Orleans, he knew of Frank Sweeny's claim to the Lafont land by virtue of an old letter of agreement and he was saddened to have to be a part of it. He had made his meeting room available for the transaction and the Lafont women were seated around a large table, dressed in their finest clothing. Caroline had not told her mother everything. She had said only that the situation was well in hand and had told them not to worry. Luke knew everything but he kept quiet.

Simon Newcomb sat at the head of the table and looked up at the wall clock. It was two minutes before two.

"Maybe Mr. Sweeny has changed his mind," young Joelle Lafont suggested.

"No," Newcomb said. "Unless I miss my guess, he will walk in at the stroke of two."

Newcomb was correct. As the clock struck the first tone, Frank Sweeny stepped through the door of the meeting room dressed formally in a coat and vest. He crossed his arms in front of him and looked at Caroline and her family.

"It is good to see all of you," he said, "though it saddened me to learn of Henri's death." Frank pulled out his letter of agreement. "But business is business and I do have this letter in which Henri and I agreed to leave all our holdings to each other in the event one of us should die. As Henri was tragically killed in the heroic defense of the Alamo, I hereby call in the agreement."

"You spoke about compensation?" Caroline suggested.

"Uh, yes," Frank said. He hedged a bit. "You understand that I am not obliged to pay you anything. Times have been difficult and I am short of money, now. But, I will pay one hundred dollars for your share of the property."

"One hundred dollars? Our land is worth fifty times that," Caroline said.

"But I'm under no obligation to pay you anything," Frank repeated, waving his finger at her.

"Mr. Newcomb, I understand my father has a safety deposit box here," Caroline said.

"Yes, that is true," Newcomb said.

"If you will look in the box, you will discover another letter of agreement, entered into and signed by both my father and Mr. Sweeny, in which this original letter is voided."

"Your father's box is locked and we would have to get a court order to open it," Newcomb said.

Caroline produced the key.

"My father told me where to find his key," she said. "Now, if you would get the box for us?"

"No!" Sweeny said. "How do we know she didn't put the letter in the box?"

"Mr. Sweeny," Newcomb said, "we keep excellent records which would stand up in any court in the land. Our records indicate that no one has touched this box in over a year. If there is such a letter, I assure you, Henri Lafont himself put it there."

Sweeny fidgeted nervously until the box was produced. Newcomb, using the key Caroline had given him, as well as the corresponding key held by the bank, opened the box. It took only a moment to find the letter that relieved the family of the necessity of selling out to Sweeny. As Caroline, her mother, and her sisters were hugging each other happily, Frank Sweeny suddenly grabbed another document from the safety box and started toward the door with it.

Luke reached him in three quick steps and held his arms. "What did you take from the box?" he demanded.

"Nothing," Sweeny whined. "Let me go!"

Luke squeezed Sweeny's arms so tightly that Sweeny cried out in pain and the envelope he held dropped to the floor as Sweeny rubbed his wrist gingerly.

"It's just a document of no significance," Sweeny mumbled.

"Mr. Sweeny, it is a felony to take anything from this box without permission," Newcomb said.

Luke retrieved the envelope, opened it, then chuckled and handed it to Caroline, who read the paper carefully.

"So, you were going to buy us out for one hundred dollars, were you?" Caroline said.

"Each," Frank said. "One hundred dollars for each of you."

"Yes, I'm sure you intended it to be that way," Caroline said. "Mother, I don't think we will ever have to worry about Mr. Sweeny again. According to this agreement, he owes us ten thousand dollars. He must pay us that money by May thirtieth or forfeit all his claims to our land."

"May thirtieth?"

"That was three days ago," Caroline said. "Do you have the money, Mr. Sweeny?"

"Uh, no," Frank mumbled. "I've had some reverses."

"Mr. Sweeny, what you tried to do here today is criminal," Newcomb said. "If these good people so wished, you could be confined to prison."

"Please," Sweeny begged. "Be merciful."

Caroline looked at Sweeny and sighed. At one time, there must have been some good in him. Otherwise, her father would have never entered into a business partnership with him.

"Very well," she said. "I want you to sign over all your interest in the plantation to my mother and my sisters."

"The sugar mill, too?"

"You may keep the sugar mill," Caroline said. "I am interested only in the plantation."

"I'll do it," Frank agreed. "Give me the papers."

"You must also promise never to bother my mother or my sisters again," Caroline said. "Because if you do, I'll come back for you."

"I'll do anything you say," Frank agreed. "Please, don't prosecute."

———

CAROLINE AND LUKE spent two weeks with her mother. Then, after a tearful farewell, she and Luke boarded a schooner in New Orleans for their trip back to Galveston.

It was dusk by the time the schooner cleared the headwaters of the Mississippi and headed out into the Gulf. Caroline stood at the rail in Luke's arms, watching as the last strips of color faded from the western sky.

"You don't mind returning to Texas?" Luke asked.

Caroline smiled up at him. "You are my husband, Luke Calhoun. Wherever you go, I will go—wherever you die, I will die."

"We've seen enough dying to last us a lifetime, Caroline," Luke said. "Let's have no talk of it."

"There's a good way to keep me from talking," Caroline teased.

"Oh? And how is that, my love?"

"Like this," she said, putting her arms around his neck and drawing his lips down to hers. The kiss grew deeper and they clung to each other passionately. Finally, Caroline pulled away. "Do you understand now?"

"I do indeed," Luke said.

"You know where this ship be headed?" they heard someone on deck call.

"Sure I do," another answered. "We're goin' to Texas."

"It ain't just Texas anymore," the first voice replied. "It's the United States of Texas."

"Ain't no such thing. It's the Republic of Texas," someone else said.

"Well, whatever it is, there's gonna be some excitin' times there, I reckon," the first voice said.

"Lord, I hope not," Luke mumbled with a laugh. "I've had about all the excitement I can handle."

"Luke?" Caroline asked hesitantly.

"Yes."

"Do you think the people will remember what has happened? Did the men of the Alamo buy anything more than a moment of glory?"

"Caroline, a hundred years from now, no one will ever have heard of you or me. But men like your pa, Ben Nichols, Almeron Dickinson, Jim Bowie, and William Barret Travis? They'll live forever. Don't you worry. As long as there is a Texas, people will remember the Alamo."

TAKE A LOOK AT: IRON HORSE
BY ROBERT VAUGHAN

FROM NEW YORK TIMES BEST-SELLING AUTHOR ROBERT VAUGHAN COMES A WESTERN FICTION NOVEL OF DETERMINATION, OBSTACLES, AND LOVE.

Gabe Hansen is determined to build a railroad from Albuquerque to the Pacific Ocean, but first, he must deal with two major adversaries.

One is Bernardo Tafoya, a Mexican who does all he can to prevent the railroad from coming through land that his family holds by virtue of an old Spanish land grant. The other obstacle to the railroad is Peter Van Zandt, son of Emory Van Zandt, the financier who is backing the railroad. Peter wants to get control of the railroad for himself.

Makenna O'Shea is a beautiful young woman who becomes a surprisingly strong ally, falling in love with Gabe in the process. Makenna is forced to make a decision that saves the railroad, but at the expense of her relationship with Gabe.

AVAILABLE NOW

THANK YOU

Thank you for taking the time to read *The Battle for Texas*. If you enjoyed it, please consider telling your friends or posting a short review. Word of mouth is an author's best friend and much appreciated.

Thank you.

Robert Vaughan

ABOUT THE AUTHOR

Robert Vaughan sold his first book when he was 19. That was 57 years and nearly 500 books ago. His books have hit the NYT bestseller list seven times. He has won the Spur Award, the PORGIE Award (Best Paperback Original), the Western Fictioneers Lifetime Achievement Award, received the Readwest President's Award for Excellence in Western Fiction, is a member of the American Writers Hall of Fame and is a Pulitzer Prize nominee.

Vaughan is also a retired army officer, helicopter pilot with three tours in Vietnam. And received the Distinguished Flying Cross, the Purple Heart, The Bronze Star with three oak leaf clusters, the Air Medal for valor with 35 oak leaf clusters, the Army Commendation Medal, the Meritorious Service Medal, and the Vietnamese Cross of Gallantry.

Made in the USA
Columbia, SC
17 May 2025

58081855R00164